ANTICIPATION

First Published in Great Britain 2018 by Mirador Publishing

Copyright © 2018 by Ralph Bland

All rights reserved. No part of this publication may be reproduced or transmitted, in any form or by any means, without permission of the publishers or author. Excepting brief quotes used in reviews.

First edition: 2018

Any reference to real names and places are purely fictional and are constructs of the author. Any offence the references produce is unintentional and in no way reflects the reality of any locations or people involved.

A copy of this work is available through the British Library.

ISBN: 978-1-912601-17-2

Mirador Publishing
10 Greenbrook Terrace
Taunton
Somerset
TA1 1UT
UK

Anticipation

By

Ralph Bland

*"On the tongue on the eyes on the ears in the palms of one's hands –
There is more than glass between the snow and the huge roses."*

"SNOW"

Louis MacNeice

ONE
6:45, Thursday morning
Valentine's Day
Sullivan, Tennessee

For a change, everyone had made it in to work this morning. No one was running late or wasting time filling his ear with a lot of excuses about having to get off early because of the holiday or any of the usual crap like that that usually went on, but even with everything going along so smoothly Ray Jenkins still had a bad feeling about the upcoming day. He'd been up at four and at work since just after five this morning, and the longer he stayed at it getting things done and not seeing anything going wrong or anybody going about their morning jobs in a way that was going to screw everything up later on then the more he kept feeling absolutely convinced that his luck was going to run out and how very soon the entire operation of the store would be off the track like a big train wreck without any way possible of getting the locomotive and all the cars rolling again. It was in his head and he couldn't shake it, but he kept reminding himself this was the way he felt every morning and none of this that was in his head now was any different from that. This was just a holiday, he told himself, and he always tended to freak out on holidays. He'd been doing it regularly for a quite a few years now.

But at least this holiday was only Valentine's Day. Nothing too major about that. It wasn't like it was the day before Easter or Thanksgiving or Christmas Eve or any of the really big boys. It wasn't even the Saturday before the Super Bowl—that had been two weeks ago—and nothing had been all that bad that day either. There'd been some employee call-outs of course, and the damned vendors hadn't left enough chips and beer to make it all the way through to kickoff, but it still hadn't resulted in anything earth-shattering or anywhere close to denoting the end of the world financially or customer-relations wise. Like every holiday that brought in extra business and demanded extra help be around to take care of the crush, the time always passed and zero hour (Thanksgiving, Christmas, Easter) arrived and then it was over and everybody—including himself—lived through it. There may have been a few hurt feelings and wounded egos around his employee base but sooner or later everybody got over it. As a matter of fact, it seemed like he was generally the only one who suffered anything too deep to recover from during these little ordeals. When they were over he would make notes about what had happened and type them in on his computer at home, thinking he could look them over a year from now and somehow avoid the misfortune and bad decisions that had come to roost this time around, but somehow he never seemed to glean too much from the notes when he read them later on after the fact.

What was bothering him so much this morning was the fact that no amount of prepared notes in the world could help him through this holiday if the inevitable cloud hanging over the city actually came to fruition. He could re-read his musings from Valentine's Day last year and see the floral sales and the candy purchases and the greeting cards from Non-Food and he still wouldn't know the first way to turn this time around. Last year it had been forty-five degrees and overcast all day, but that was all. It was the kind of weather no one noticed, weather that didn't stop anybody from doing anything. But this year no one really knew. It was cold outside. There was a big cloud cover, the weathermen all said, three channels of smiling trustworthy local meteorologists jointly shrugging their shoulders and saying there just might be the chance of snow sometime. It all depends on this front, they all said, and they pointed at it with their remotes and their handhelds like it was something from another world that had just touched down and they didn't know quite what to make of it just yet. But we are watching it closely, they said, smiling their reassuring smiles. We'll keep you informed.

He comes up front to make sure everything is ready for opening and sees Bob and Lyle leaning on the office ledge talking to Martha through the plexiglass window. This is nothing new in the morning, since his head butcher and number one grocery clerk do this at the start of each day as part of their daily routine, like it is some kind of requirement, but right now it irritates Ray to the ultimate core of himself seeing it, since he's having all sorts of trepidations about all that could and probably will go wrong today while his three highest paid employees here see fit to laugh and joke and flirt and fairly well pay no attention to the seriousness this coming day might require as far as effort and planning. He wants to go over and break this gathering up right this instant, but this is not the way he does things, so he swallows his feelings and lets them collect with everything else churning and bubbling in his stomach and goes over and begins facing the loaves of bread on the bread rack, even though Derrick will be in at seven and will start performing this task all over again.

Speaking of Derrick, Ray sees him through the locked front door leaning on the railing, smoking a cigarette and examining the sports page to see if the Pacers won last night. Derrick is from Terre Haute or somewhere around there, and he acts as if a regular season basketball game that means nothing in the grand scheme of things is truly the most important thing in the world. Well, Ray amends, maybe the second most important thing. Women and how he can get them to go to bed with him would of course top Derrick's list every time. Ray knew. He'd been watching Derrick go through his paces for the last dozen or so years. Not too much had changed over that time.

Lillian walks up to the door with a cup of coffee in one hand and her purse in the other and a long Virginia Slim hanging from her lips like an albino ice pick. She wraps on the door with her car keys, a sharp staccato clicking sound that irritates Ray a little more each day, since he always sees Lillian there and is always on his way to unlock the door to let her in when she starts in with her pecking. He knows she sees him coming, but she raps with her keys anyway, and it's all he can do to keep from saying anything when he gets there and turns the latch and she and Derrick slide inside.

"Morning," is the only thing that escapes his mouth.

"Morning, Ray," she says back.

"Hey," says Derrick.

"We're going to get busy here in a little," Ray says. "People are going to be in here buying cards and candy and flowers for

Valentine's and be all worried about getting snowed in at the same time. Nobody knows if it's going to actually snow or not."

"Even if it does snow it ain't going to be anything big," Derrick says. "People act like two or three inches is something to get worried about. Shoot, they ought to try living in Indiana for a winter. They'd see what snow's all about if they did."

"People don't know how to drive in it is what makes it so bad." Lyle Randalls has abandoned window-talking with Martha and Bob and moved over to look out the front door and talk to Ray. "A little white stuff starts falling from the sky and they think they have to get in their cars and go out and run into somebody. Things would be a whole lot better if everybody would just stay home a day or two and let things melt. It's not like everybody has to get out on the street at the same time."

There are three cars that pull into the lot in succession, and Ray goes ahead and cuts on the power switch at the top of the doors, even though it's still five minutes until seven. He knows Lillian won't be back up front until after seven, until she's clocked in and walked around and said hello to everybody and stuck her nose in the meat department to share some gossip with Shirley Hoover, who can't work and talk at the same time, so she has to lean on her wrapping machine and talk to Lillian and let the rail stack up with meat to be priced while the two of them let production come to a complete halt. He tries not to think about it. Ray straightens some paper bags on the check stand and says hello to the customers as they walk in and get bascarts. Nobody seems to be after just one thing. Everybody looks like they intend to stock up.

Ray wonders if they've changed the forecast since the last time he checked.

On the back dock Derrick stops before going up front to the bread rack to burn another cigarette with Marcus and Larry. Marcus Treadway works in the meat department as a cutter, but since Shirley is busy talking with Lillian everything he and Lyle have cut and wrapped is jammed up on the conveyor and there's no more room to add the sirloin tips he's been working on, so taking a smoke while Lyle isn't around seems like the thing to do. Marcus knows Lyle. He's up front sucking up to Ray like he does most every morning, so it's not like there's any rush to get anything else accomplished.

Larry Jones is careful about taking too much time or disappearing away from his job, so he tends to hotbox his Newport and get back to what he was doing before it gets discovered he's gone missing. Bob, who's over him and tells him what to do all day so his own lazy ass won't have to work too hard, is up front trying to get in Martha Perry's pants, which Larry knows isn't ever going to happen, and even if it did goddamn cracker Bob wouldn't know what to do with it anyway. Larry doesn't worry about it much, since he figures this shit's been going on before he got here and isn't going to stop anytime soon. It's been going on long before he, Larry, broke into a church in Camden and got locked up almost a year because he took some money the church had designated for an orphans' home. White Church of Christ assholes, they were. Absolutely the wrong people to lift anything from. He'd fucked up. If he'd broke and entered any other place he'd probably had gotten off with almost no jail time at all, but with the Church of Christs he got hit as hard as they could make it. Eleven months and twenty-nine days, not one day off for good behavior or it being his first big offense or nothing. Hell, he was lucky just to get a job after that shit. The workhouse ministry set him up with this and made it a point to tell him how, if he fucked up again, he'd be hard-pressed to ever find a good job again. He was twenty years old, he was a high school dropout, and he was black. He had a tendency to believe they were right.

Ray doesn't have to check out anybody before Lillian makes it to the front, because even old Steve who comes in every morning for a honey bun and a pack of Winstons isn't ready to instantaneously check out this morning; he's on his way to the back for some lunch meat and potato chips, after having already picked up a loaf of bread when he first grabbed his honey bun. Ray notices how Steve has two honey buns this morning instead of his customary one, so maybe Steve is expecting something bad coming his way too.

The city bus closes its doors with a hiss and Paulette Price comes in the door an hour early. Ray is all prepared to tell her not to clock in early the way she likes to do to earn a few extra dollars every week, but he thinks of how she could maybe fill the eggs up high before it gets too awfully busy, so he decides to wait and let her clock in and then assign her that job as an afterthought. It won't be what she likes to do—Paulette likes to straighten the greeting card rack and look at the morning paper while she's doing it—so maybe this way Ray can get something off his back and send her a little message too about how she really isn't allowed to do just anything she wants to around here. He's not stupid, though. He knows his lessons like this never take with anyone much. That's the way it is when you've got people who've been around for a while, he thinks. After a certain period of time they just tune you out and start doing whatever they want. They know they'll get away with it. They all know Ray isn't the kind of guy who's ever going to actually fire anybody.

He knows it too. It's not that he hasn't ever fired an employee here at Ray's Bargain Foods, but it's been a few years since he's had to. A dozen years, probably, but he remembers it like yesterday. It was a high school girl who ran a cash register a couple of nights a week and weekends, and her boyfriend who worked back in the store keeping the meat counter and the produce rack and the dairy department filled up and cleaned up. They were both good kids, he'd believed, and he had no reason not to trust them, but things started coming up missing and inventories didn't look good. He started circling the parking lot at nights sometime and coming in the back when nobody knew it and hiding upstairs to watch what was going on. He saw the two of them open the back door up and take some bags outside- steaks and roasts and hams hidden back along the corner of the store- and he saw people go through the girl's check lane (Linda was her name, he still remembered her, she was a pretty girl) and nothing much would get rung up. The boy would come from the back and help bag the groceries and take them out to the person's car. The person shopping was just a kid too. It turned out they all went to school together and they were selling groceries and meat cheap to anybody who wanted to buy them. The police were really the ones who caught them. Ray already knew what was going on when they came to tell him, but it made it easier to fire them that way, since they'd already been caught and arrested. Sometimes he wonders these days is if it had been left up to him if he would have given them both another chance. He's not sure if the answer is Yes or No.

There's a part of him that wants to look out at the lot and see if Lee has managed to make it into work yet. He hasn't seen him come through the front door, but that doesn't really hold any water as to determining his presence in the store or not, since, when he's late—which is almost all the time—Lee likes to sneak through the back door when he thinks no one is looking and start doing something at the produce rack like he's already been at work for quite a while. Of course this never works with Ray, since he knows how sneaky and undependable his oldest son can be. He knows if the boy is here or not. If he doesn't spot him off the bat all he really has to do is check his time card to see what time he got in, even though Lee got used to him doing that, so after a while he started acting like he'd forgotten to hit the clock when he came in the first thing in the morning--he was either too sleepy to remember or thinking too much about a display he was going to build a little later-- and it escaped his mind. This never worked with Ray, on account he knew his son too well. He knew where his mind was. Girls, alcohol, what drugs he could afford to buy, that was what was up there, and not a whole lot else.

As much as he is surprised to see him, it's not that Ray is overjoyed when he spots Lee over by the banana table bagging up the ripest of the stock to sell as reduced. Lee has that vacant expression on his face Ray is growing accustomed to, and Ray can tell Lee is paying absolutely no attention to the quality or amount of bananas he is stuffing into each paper bag. It's bad enough that some of the customers like to slip another half or three quarters pound into the reduced bags as they're grabbing them off the table and thinking no one is looking and no one will notice at the register, but for Lee to stuff each bag twice as full as it should be and cut off any chance for a reasonable profit irks Ray to the core, especially when he has told Lee time and time again how much to put in each bag. It just goes to show how much Lee, and to tell the truth, everybody else who works here, half listens to anything he tells them.

"Don't stuff them so full, Lee," he says as he passes by. "You know what I told you about cutting into your profit."

"Okay, Dad,' Lee answers, almost as if he might give a shit.

Ray has lapped the store once now and wants to go back into his office downstairs and catch the weather forecast again to see what the forecasters are saying now, but he's already seen the Coke truck pulling around to the back receiving door, and he knows he needs to get back there so the vendors can get in early and get done on the floor stocking before the store gets too filled with customers. He glances over toward the first aisle and sees it may be too late for that already. There's a logjam of women pushing bascarts and piling stuff high in them, so he doesn't really need to hear a forecast again to know that somebody's predicting something is going to happen. It may just be an inch or two of snow, but this is the South, this is Tennessee, and that's enough to get people all stirred up. This town may be a lot smaller and more rural than the big cities of Memphis and Nashville, but it's not like everybody lives on a farm and can provide for themselves during bad weather. They have to get to a store in case it gets bad. It hardly ever does, Ray knows, for he's been around this town of Sullivan almost his entire life, but every now and then it will surprise you. He remembers times when it has.

Bread, milk, and toilet paper, he thinks. Here we go. The

notion of what is fixing to happen almost makes him grin. Sometimes you just have to have a sense of humor when you're about to get your ass kicked.

The vendors know what's getting ready to transpire and do their best to load up their sections in a hurry. Ray has to keep his eye on the King Brothers Snacks driver, since he's caught him a couple of times with miscounts on his pies and cakes, calling them eight when they're seven perhaps, or maybe even six. The guy is quick to say sorry and admit his error, likes to pass it off as something that happens because he is not so good at math, but Ray knows this probably isn't the truth. He's seen the guy figure his ticket without a calculator, so a lack of mathematical skill certainly isn't the foremost problem.

Ray is in the middle of checking in several vendors when he hears Martha on the intercom. She is calling for all additional help to come to the front end, and Ray knows by those words that the checkout lines have stretched and elongated into far more than Lillian and Paulette can handle. He is at least glad Paulette came in early, for if she hadn't he'd be stuck with only one checker right now. He only has two more checklanes he can open, and the only ones who can check are Martha—who'll have to leave the office unattended—and himself, so he'd better get these vendors out of the way and get up front as fast as possible. He reaches over for the telephone on the wall and punches the button for an outside line. It's early and Trent has to close tonight, but right this minute he needs to have all hands on deck. Trent can check if he has to. He'd call some of the other checkers in if he could, but they're all in school this moment. Maybe school will let out early and he can get a couple of them to come in then.

Martha can't stand the sight of Larry and Bob and Lee and Derrick all standing behind Lillian and Paulette waiting for something to slide down the conveyor belt before they can bag it. Martha knows she is twice as fast as both Lillian and Paulette put together—she is lightning when she opens up a register, scans those orders through in the flash of an eye—so she makes sure the safe is locked and the cash drawer fastened and comes out of the office to open up the first register. Probably, she thinks, if she had been the only checker out on the floor when this rush began she could have kept the lines down by herself, but this is just the way it is with Lillian and Paulette. Sometimes they try to outdo each other seeing who can be the slowest. Martha knows it's almost close to impossible to be as slow as these two without trying very hard to be that way.

Of course, as soon as she begins to check the phone starts ringing and a woman comes to the window to send a Western Union. Martha keeps on checking. She could have predicted this. She just hopes Ray will get himself up front in the next minute or two. It's not going to be good if he gets stuck on the back door and can't get away.

Lee leans against the plastic bag rack and watches Larry bag the order Paulette is sending toward him a little at a time. It is stupid for him to stand here, but he'll get in trouble with his dad if he leaves and goes back to the Produce department after Martha has called him to the front. Besides, if he goes back there he might get stuck unloading a truck or doing some other crap-ass job his dad might find for him to do. It's probably best to stand here and take a little break. God knows he needs it.

He's lucky to even be here this morning. He was out pretty late with some of his buddies last night, and it was going on two before he got into bed. At least he thinks that's what time it was. He remembers looking at the clock by the bed and not having it totally register in his mind. He was pretty blown away, let's face it. He'd done good just moving the little lever so the alarm would go off, then he'd completed the miracle by actually hearing the buzzer when it went off and getting out of bed without ignoring the sound like he does so many mornings and going back to sleep. He knew his dad was going to be here this morning, so he made himself get up and be here. There could have been some real trouble if he hadn't. There have been a few mornings his dad has driven home from the store and come into the bedroom and shook him awake. Lee can do without that kind of shit the first thing in the morning.

So he had whiskey and beer and some blow and a little weed last night. He'd had a good buzz, but it wasn't as wasted a feeling as he'd had a few times before here lately. The good thing was he wasn't having to go out in his own car and look for some action every night and having to take the chance of getting busted by the police. He had some friends who didn't mind coming by and picking him up in the afternoons after work and then bringing him back home long after everybody in the house—his dad and mom, his little sisters—had gone to bed for the night, so most of the time he didn't have to fuck with anybody when he got in. There'd been that night six weeks ago when the cops had stopped him driving home from a party and got him on a DUI, which was bad because he'd had to call his dad to bail him out, but was good at least in the sense that he didn't have any drugs or shit on him or stashed in the car anywhere. The DUI was bad enough, especially here in Sullivan, this fucking hick town where everybody knows everything about everybody else, but at least all it ended up being was a weekend sleeping in a dorm and picking up trash down by the park and having his license suspended for a year. Now all he can supposedly do is drive his car to work, but he thinks in a month or so he can start getting around that a little. In the meantime, he can keep bumming rides off his friends.

"Slow down, man," he grins at Larry. "It ain't like you're going to get a raise for bagging so fast today. You keep this pace up and you'll make me look bad, like I'm a complete jerk-off or something."

"Jerk-off's your middle name," Larry says. He keeps his eyes on the counter and doesn't slow down. He needs to keep this job, and this fucking white cracker Lee makes him nervous. He can see himself getting fired just because of something this asshole gets him into. "Just cause your daddy ain't about to chew you out over anything don't mean it ain't going to happen to me instead. He could get pissed off at you and take it out on my ass in your fucking place."

Lee laughs. He thinks stuff like this is funny.

Ray finally gets the back door clear and pulls down the sliding door and bolts it. He steps out the regular door and takes a look at the sky one last time before locking it and walking to the front at a brisk pace. Ray is the fastest walker on the face of the earth and gets kidded about it often. Down through the years employees have had a good old time imitating his walk, scooting through the backroom or up the aisles with their elbows chugging like they are in the Olympics and this is the final contest that determines who will get the gold medal. Walking like Ray around the store is always the source for a good laugh. Ray knows it goes on and has known about it for years, but he doesn't get self-conscious about it. He knows he acquired this skill honestly, mimicking his former manager at the old Wilson Brothers' Grocery just off the interstate. It was 1968 then, and Billy Wilson hired him on as a favor to his daddy. Ray didn't want to disappoint anybody with his performance then—his dad, Billy or Joel Wilson, or Danny Forest, who was this fellow a few years out of high school and back from the service in Viet Nam who worked back in the dairy and all over the store—and Ray had done everything he could to be dependable and do a good job and get whatever job he got assigned to do not only completed but finished up in record time. He'd picked that up from Danny, who'd been a halfback on the football team and All Region in basketball and run the 100 yard dash when he was in high school. Ray had seen him play football and basketball a few times back then, and as a boy he'd begun idolizing Danny. So when Ray got hired at Wilson Brothers' and saw Danny was working there and that he was his helper and assistant he made up his mind right then he was going to be just like Danny in everything he did. He worked his tail off in those days, and when he finished one job he made sure he got in a big hurry to move on to the next one waiting. People used to smile at him and tell him to slow down, but he just kept on moving. He wanted to make sure he kept up with Danny.

He gets to the front in time to cash a pay check and get a Western Union sent. The lines are not as bad as he'd imagined they would be, and he looks down and sees Martha checking like a whirlwind and knows he can thank her for the front end not being totally swamped. There's still one check lane he could open if he had anyone here who could check besides himself, but he hasn't been able to find a good candidate he could throw into a register in an emergency situation like this. That's why he's been trying to call Trent in, but there's been no answer so far. That's the way it is with Trent, though. There isn't any telling where he might be at this time of the morning, whose bed he might be sleeping in.

"You fellows better get some carts in," he tells Larry and Lee and Derrick. "Ya'll are about to let them get empty."

"I just filled them up a couple of minutes ago," Derrick says. "There ain't no more left outside to get."

At last count Ray had fifty-two bascarts in his inventory, so to look at his inside rack and see one sitting there isn't a very good sign to him. He walks out of the office and goes out the door to look for himself. Derrick is right. Except for one cart parked way down at the end of the lot there's nothing to see but cars and cars filling up all the parking spaces he'd just finished repainting last week. To save money he'd got out there with James and done it himself. He guesses it's a good thing he'd got it done now. If he hadn't there might be cars parked every which way all over. It was hard enough to get in and out on a regular basis—this old lot wasn't made for too much traffic.

It had its share of traffic right now, he saw, and it was only going to get worse as the day progressed. He looked at the sky, all gray and black. Except for the sound of cars going back and forth on the street and pulling steadily into the lot, the rest of the world seemed quiet and hushed, like it was waiting and listening for something coming from somewhere it couldn't quite pinpoint or understand.

It was coming up on eight o'clock on Valentine's Day morning.

TWO
8:00 A.M.

Trent Collier rarely heard his cell phone ringing when he was sleeping. It wasn't that he was deaf or that heavy of a sleeper or anything like that, but it was more from the fact that when he coasted off to sleep and was safe and tucked away in his goodbye mode he was like a broadcasting station that has signed off the air after a day's activities and there is no one around to punch a button or give the forecast or play a record or anything. The watts were reduced, the lights were out, the doors were locked, there was no one at work. Whatever anybody wanted was just too bad. They would have to wait until later.

This morning Trent didn't have any trouble hearing his phone making its *Mission Impossible* ring tone, because he'd been awake since Martha left just after five. She'd run home to take a quick shower and dress and be at work at 6:30, something that had never happened in the first three months of their relationship before. The fact that she had actually spent the night at his condo without worrying if her husband would discover her missing from home kept running through Trent's mind like one of those stock cars down at the county racetrack, going round and round and making a real roaring sound in his ears where he couldn't concentrate on anything else.

So he heard the phone ringing loud and clear, but he didn't want to look and see who it might be because of the possibility the identity of the caller might freak him out even more. At this time of the morning he assumed it was probably the store calling—Martha to report she'd made it on time or Ray to talk to him about the possible snow scare that may or may not be happening today. Trent didn't want to talk to Martha so soon and he didn't want to listen to Ray having a hemorrhage over an inch of snow getting ready to fall, and he for damned sure didn't want to look at his phone and see it was someone else calling him so early in the morning. The image of Martha's husband came to his mind, good old Pete, patrolman down at the Sullivan Police Department, with his shaved head and his Fu Manchu mustache and his hundred extra pounds on Trent that might get used to full advantage if he ever happened to find out what Trent and his wife had been up to lately. So Trent decided it wouldn't hurt for him to keep on lounging in bed and put off whatever emergency the world was attempting to send his way at eight o'clock in the morning.

This is Trent's second year working at Ray's Bargain Foods. He sort of lucked into this job as co-manager when the local beer distributor hooked on with Anheuser-Busch and he got let go as a route salesman because the Bud folks thought they had enough drivers to absorb all of Andrews Distributing's routes with their own people. Trent had worked for Andrews three years by then, but was still making a little less than jackshit on his salary and commissions, generally because Andrews carried in their inventory a lot of different kinds of beer that nobody in the town of Sullivan much cared to drink. There were no big-name brands like Budweiser or Miller or Coors in his truck, only unheard-of titles like Moss's Ale or Pal's beer or Murphy's Irish Delight, so Trent could usually make all his stops and be off shortly after lunch and have time to go to a couple of rotating bars around town and sample a few brands himself and try to pick up loose women who might be hanging about the premises waiting for somebody like him to come along and start the process.

The hours were good for his social life but his salary wasn't substantial enough to support it, and so when Andrews got absorbed and his job became reduced to a memory Trent was left with the conflicting sensations of despair and ire for being suddenly jobless and relief and gratitude because he didn't have to load a truck every morning and ride around town sweating and risking hurting his back for what amounted to peanuts on the pay scale. He'd delivered to Ray's as a beer vendor for a while and heard a few times how Ray was looking for help, so he'd dusted off his personality and his best bar-hopping clothes and gone in to apply for a job. He tried not to show too much desperation in his interview, and either he succeeded in doing so or Ray was by this time desperate enough himself for help, and Trent got hired right off the bat. He didn't truly think it was going to be the answer to his prayers, but it would do for a while. Trent only believed in prayer for the times when he was really fucked up for certain, and he wasn't all that far gone at that point. He was just moving from quicksand to dry land. Ray's Bargain Foods looked like a good place to catch his breath at for a while.

He hadn't planned on what was going on between him and

Martha to progress to quite the point it was now. He had, after all, kept his distance from her for almost a year when he first started working at Ray's, categorizing her as a well-preserved woman at least seven years older than him who laughed and casually flirted and knew how to laugh and what to say to men to have things go her way. He'd seen women like her before. He'd also seen her husband when he came in the store for anything. He knew about him too. He was a cop, and he wasn't the kind of policeman a fellow like Trent wanted to get on the bad side of. He heard plenty of talk from Lyle and Bob about how jealous Pete Perry was, so Trent didn't want to have anything to do with that end of the stick.

But there was something about Martha that wouldn't let him keep his distance. She became like a magnet to his imagination, and he found himself drawing nearer and nearer to her a little at a time, ignoring what his good sense kept telling him.

The phone began to ring again, and Trent Collier turned over on his side and looked at the wall for a while.

THREE
9:00 A.M.

The first flakes start falling just after the rush hour finishes and everybody is where they're all supposed to be, whether this is at work or at home or at school, but from the looks of the people milling in the aisles and jamming up the front end Ray can tell not much of anything is going to stay normal for too much longer now. All he has to do is look out the window at the fat white snowflakes beginning to fill the air, and he knows the onslaught is not only going to continue but is fixing to get progressively worse.

It's going to be a long day. He knows it. He hopes everybody else does too.

The front end rush dies down momentarily, long enough for Martha to make her way out of the check lane and back inside the office to finish her morning books. Ray has seen all the checks and money and credit slips spread out on her desk just right of the office window, but he hasn't dared touch or move anything or try to help in any way. He knows better than this from way back. Martha has her own system that she half-borrowed from when she used to work at Piggly Wiggly and half invented herself, sort of a best of two worlds type of operation. Six or seven years ago she tried teaching it to Ray, but after a few minutes they both came to the agreement that it was impossible. Ray could count money all day—he was well-versed in that—but what he couldn't do was add up checks and make them match to perfection to go to the bank for deposit. First of all, his fingers were too stiff and immobile to run a calculator the way Martha could. Also, he possessed little patience when it came to looking through the paperwork and computer entries for errors of dollars and cents. He couldn't understand all the checks and balances Martha had installed in her bookkeeping system to insure accuracy. She had no trouble teaching the process to the part-timers hired in to keep things straight during the evenings, and Trent and Paulette had learned enough to halfway relieve her when she took her two days off each week, but Ray was a lost cause. He was just one of those people not made for this sort of work.

Speaking of Trent, Ray had just finished calling him for about the tenth time. He decided to give up trying to get him in and instead go back to the back office and see what the status of the school system was. He was hoping they'd get scared and dismiss early and he could get a couple of the part-time checkers to come in and run his other available registers, but he wasn't so sure how lucky he was going to get with that and wondered if there was anything else he could do to keep from getting his clock cleaned the rest of the day.

The phone rang again and he answered it, not believing it was Trent calling back when he heard his voice.

"I was trying to get some sleep," Trent said, "but the phone kept ringing and I figured it was you. What's going on? Did we get robbed or something?"

"You ought to look out the window or turn on the TV sometime. It's starting to snow. The store's busy as hell and I can't get anybody in here to help us take care of it. I thought I'd wake you up and get you in early. Right now I'm desperate. We're in bad shape."

"I guess you know I ain't had but about two hours sleep right now."

"It's not my fault you don't know how to go to bed at night. You ought to get yourself in the sack at a decent hour like I do."

"It's not my fault I happen to have a social life." Trent rubs his eyes and peeks out his blinds at what's happening outside. "God," he says, "you really aren't lying, are you? It is snowing. I bet if I stand here for five minutes or so I can count ten flakes before I quit."

"It may not be snowing much out your way," Ray said, "but it's coming down pretty good here. It's not enough to call it a blizzard, but it's more than enough to get everybody excited. They're in here already, about like flies on shit."

Ray paused for a moment, listening to himself and his vocabulary. He wondered what it was about him when he had even the slightest conversation with Trent. He very rarely cursed, but five minutes with Trent made him come out sounding like he'd served a couple of stints in the Merchant Marines. He had this brief memory of getting in trouble at school when he was a boy. His teacher and his mother had agreed the little boy who sat across from him in class was a bad influence, and the plan jointly agreed upon was that Ray and the other little boy would be separated. Their seats would be moved to where they were not together much at all. It would be better for Ray not to be around him. Ray wondered if so much was true again in his life. Maybe Trent was a bad influence on him now. It sounded stupid to think such a thing, seeing how Trent was sometimes lazy and undependable and his ethics weren't exactly the highest Ray had ever encountered from someone else. Ray would no more want to be in Trent's position than move out of town and go to work for some company where he had no voice in any business decision whatsoever. From all he'd gathered over the past three years, there was just so much uncertainty in Trent's life almost all the time, some manner of chaos and trouble always looming either on the horizon or attempting to catch up with him from some unnamed incident in the past that Ray sometimes wondered when he was leaving work and headed for home leaving Trent in charge if that moment might be the last time he saw him. It was like there was always some doubt in his head that Trent would endure and still be around when the next day rolled around. Ray just couldn't shake the thought that there was something about his assistant manager that was purely transitory.

He heard a shout from the front doorway that almost made him jump, like someone had fired a packet of firecrackers off behind him when he'd truly thought all the July 4 festivities were done with. He didn't know why he'd been anticipating peace at a moment like this and a place like this, but perhaps it was the momentary break in all the front end hustle and activity that had lulled him into a false sense of calm. With the woman yelling by the front bread rack—Mrs. Moseley, a regular customer—any form of tranquility he'd been enjoying was now over.

"It's coming," Mrs. Moseley announced in a decibel just shy of a screech. She had on an old overcoat over the pajamas she hadn't bothered changing before coming to shop. She looked around religiously to make certain everyone within the city limits was paying attention. "It's coming down in Arkansas right now. It's headed straight for Memphis. It'll be here before we know it. And it's going to be a bad one too—you can just bet on it."

She looked around at all the faces watching her, trying to see who was going to be foolish enough not to join her, since this was a life and death situation and people needed to be choosing which side they were on and what direction they were headed when this great horrible event came down.

"We'll be snowed in by suppertime," she said in grim finality.

Ray stared at his front end and wondered if widespread panic was fixing to break out, if his usually-dour well-behaved customers were going to riot and start looting his store. He turned to see what Martha thought about all this and discovered her standing up from her desk and all the unfinished bookwork and peering over the glass to watch what was unfolding. Ray had seen her smile before and chuckle and even giggle, but he had never heard her laugh quite so loud and long as this. He watched her take off her glasses and wipe her eyes, and he wished he could find this funny too. He wished he had a sense of humor that would allow him to be entertained while the world kicked his ass and took his name.

Jesus God Almighty, he thought. It's only nine-fifteen.

"This is going to be a crazy day," Martha said.

"A real humdinger," Ray agreed.

In the meat department Lyle was cutting and Marcus was grinding and Shirley was packaging and pricing as fast as they could, but the outside racks were emptying faster than the three of them could get anything out. Lyle wished he could call his afternoon boy in, but Randy was still in school as far as he knew. He didn't think schools would be dismissed this early in the day, with the flakes just starting to fall and no one being able to tell if it was going to stick or not. He wished Ray would come back and help them get caught up like he sometimes did, but he had seen the mess that the front end already was in, and he knew it would be a long time before Ray could leave from up there to go help somewhere else. Lyle looked down at the rail full of meat waiting to go out. Any other time what he was looking at would last at least a full day, maybe even two. Now, with the way things were going, he doubted if what he saw would hold past lunch. He'd seen a few snow scares in his time and he knew how people acted. This was not his first rodeo. He was even starting to wonder if he had enough product in the cooler to get him through until the truck came tomorrow morning. If he had time he would pick up the phone and call in and add on to the order, but right now he had to keep at it. This was not the time to stop.

Lee, who didn't know how to make a decent order and didn't intend to ever learn either, watched an old woman load two big bags of Idaho potatoes in her basket. She pivoted as sharply as her aged body could—like she was on a basketball court, for Christ's sake—and added three huge heads of cabbage to the mix. He wanted to be a smart ass and go up and ask the dumb bitch if she had enough to feed herself the next day or so but decided not to, since the way she was acting she might take him seriously and start grabbing more stuff. Not that he really gave a big hairy shit. The way he looked at it was the more everybody bought then the sooner he'd be out of things to put out and he could go home and take a little nap. He knew that wasn't going to happen, though, so he made himself stop thinking about it. He knew if he ran out of stuff back in the produce department his dad would just find something else for him to do somewhere else.

Maybe he could sneak out while nobody was looking-just go out the back door and get in his car and go home. He could say he finished everything up and was just trying to save some hours by not standing around doing nothing and getting paid for it. Maybe he could get away with some sort of bullshit like that.

He heard his dad on the P.A. calling for him to come up front, so he tossed his box-cutter into the lettuce box he'd just finished emptying and walked disgustedly and as slowly as he could toward the front end. He didn't like bagging groceries much either, and it didn't help that these assholes that shopped here didn't know how to give anybody a decent tip unless it happened to be Christmas Eve. Then they acted like they were the greatest and most generous son of a bitches in the fucking world.

Derrick Watkins knows how this is going to go, and he also knows the way he's going to handle it. It's going to be busy all day with customers and the women on the front yelling at him and wanting him to be everywhere at one time every minute that goes by, so the best way to handle that problem is to stay outside as much as possible. He can talk to the customers as he takes their orders out, stand there and smile and burn a cigarette all in the name of good customer relations, and he can duck around the front of the building and get away from the action there, maybe call a girl or two on his cell phone and arrange a little something for later on. He can let some of his customers know he's going to be at work all day, so if they want a little something to smoke later on they can come by and meet him in the lot and he can make a little money on the side. He's been doing this very thing for a long time now, and though it's been close a few times, nobody has caught him yet. He's pretty much got this down to a science after eight years. He can go out the door with a customer's order and not be back inside to bag another order for fifteen or twenty minutes easy as all get-out. Mr. Ray or Mrs. Martha or somebody can come outside looking for him after they decide he's been gone too long and they'll see him talking to a customer at a car or sweeping up some broken glass or gathering up some stray bascarts, and all they can do is walk back inside and start bagging an order themselves until he comes back in, because they see he's on his way, so it gets in their head how he hasn't really been missing as long as they thought. Besides, if it gets that busy and backed up all they do is call that crazy ass cracker Lee from Produce or Larry from Grocery to help them out, and sooner or later Trice will wander in along with some of the school kids, and when that happens and there's a bunch of them running around it gets to where they hardly remember Derrick is even around at all.

Across the street there's the Allison Funeral Home, and Derrick can see they've got a funeral fixing to happen this morning. The big silver Hearse is pulled around front and some old brother in a suit is sprinkling salt on the walkway where they carry the coffin out so the pallbearers and the mourners in attendance don't slip and fall if there's snow and ice out there and bust their asses. It's a fairly good distance down that walk to where the Hearse is parked, and then when the procession gets going everybody has to go up the hill toward the town cemetery. Sometimes they have to go to the interstate to get to another town or county, but they still have to climb the hill on Pendleton Drive. Derrick knows what can happen in the winter. That hill can get slicker than a baby's dimpled ass if the snow comes down enough.

The lot is already full and Derrick considers ducking around the corner of the building to take a quick smoke, but he reconsiders when he sees Ray stick his head out the door. There aren't any stray bascarts around the lot for him to gather, so he pushes his solitary one inside and has three women leap at him like he is a rabbit and they are hunting dogs just unleashed. Three sets of hands pull at the cart and he lets go, afraid he might get knocked down and maybe trampled in the melee. Apparently, this is the only available cart left in the store, so it is a valuable commodity. The hand basket rack is empty too, and Derrick looks at the three checkout lanes with the long lines stretching down the aisles. It seems that all the eyes are staring hopefully at him, thinking perhaps that he will walk over and open the one available lane left, but Derrick has made it a point over the years to never learn to check. Once a guy gets stuck in a cash register it becomes hard to get away as much, and then there is that fact that you get made accountable for the money you took in. The last thing in the world Derrick Watkins wanted was to be accountable for anything. Fuck that.

He got away from the bascart fight as fast as he could. There was pulling and grabbing and threatening —a lot of yelling and cursing. As he moved over to Lillian's check lane he wondered if anybody was going to actually throw a punch. He also wondered if anybody was going to be dumb enough to try and break this up. All he knew for certain was it sure as hell wasn't going to be him.

FOUR
10:30 A.M.

So many people are in the store it makes it hard to think, but Ray worries about a couple of things anyway. Of course he's worried about the long lines on the front and how, even with all the lanes open now because Trent has finally made it in, they don't seem to be making any headway on whittling them down, and he's worried about how long his shelves and the stock in the grocery department and the inventory in the meat and produce departments are going to hold up before they start running out of things. He hates thinking about what might happen this afternoon when people get off from work and come in to find everything gone. They can go to the Kroger on the other side of town, or they can go up the hill and try the Piggly Wiggly, but except for a few other piddly stores here and there that's about the extent of places to grocery shop in Sullivan. Ray didn't like to think of himself as a bigoted bastard, but if Ray's Bargain Foods hadn't been built where it was and was not in this spot where the majority of the blacks in Sullivan resided he and his operation would be one of those other piddly stores too. The fact that a high percentage of his employees are black and the fact that he carried items catering to this poor black neighborhood—like chitterlings and lottery tickets—made it where he could keep a steady stream of business going pretty much all the time, since Ray's Bargain Foods seemed to be regarded as a neighborhood fixture around this part of town. It was a place where the people in the neighborhood just always and naturally went to pick up what they needed without giving it a whole lot of thought.

But sometimes the store just wasn't quite big enough to handle what was happening at the time. That was the way it was right now, what with the crowded aisles and checkout lanes and the parking lot where cars are starting to go every which way and line up helter skelter with horns blaring and the drivers yelling at each other. These kind of situations were never frequent enough to make Ray think he needed to undertake some permanent solution to solve them, so over the years he had just learned to bear with them and suffer through them until they had run their course. But it was days like today, Valentine's Day, a non-major holiday for sure, but a day that required some advance planning and special thought, that is concerning him the most right now.

There wasn't a floral shop inside Ray's Bargain Foods. There wasn't a big greeting card rack where birthdays and Thank You cards and anniversaries could be noted. So what Ray had to deal with here on his poor side of Sullivan when a day like Valentine's rolled around was to think about getting boxes of chocolates in to put on a table up front, and he had to order Valentine cards—cheap boxes for the kids and some discounted inexpensive generic offerings to work in on a metal turnaround rack he kept in the back for such days—and mostly he had to work up a deal with his regular food distributor out of Arkansas to get roses wrapped in cellophane delivered to him on the truck before the fourteenth so he could put them up on the table by the front and sell them for extra profit too.

But things weren't working out as well as he'd like for them to right now.

He kept passing by his front end holiday display table and nothing seemed to be happening there. The chocolates resided peacefully in their boxes with the red bows around them, the metal turnaround stand stayed filled with greeting cards of love declarations and abiding adoration, and the roses in their plastic wrap all remained unflinchably present in their four neat rows beside the chocolates. If Ray had taken a picture this morning before opening of how beautiful and eye-catching his St. Valentine's display looked, this image at 10:30 in the morning was almost identical with what would have appeared to him in the frame. He could glance around and watch the bread disappearing off the rack in aisle one, he could note the carts going by laden with toilet paper and gallons of milk and all the items of fresh meat and buckets of chitterlings they could possibly hold, but nowhere was he seeing greeting cards or sweets for the sweet, or, most alarmingly, roses as a symbol of constant and eternal love.

Ray came to the conclusion that when snow was falling on the poor side of Sullivan, Tennessee, the last thing in the world any of the denizens gave much of a hoot about was romance. He had to admit that his plans to make any profit on this day devoted to romantic embellishment was being chiefly ignored and going down the tubes on this morning where everybody ascertained a blizzard was on its way and the chances were good they were going to get snowed in for weeks or starve and have to resort to cannibalism or freeze and not be discovered until the big thaw at the coming of spring. So what was the big deal about the promise of love and happiness when such a dire future fate awaited them all?

Ray could live with the greeting cards remaining on the inventory. It wasn't like they were going to go out of date and have to be discarded like pitching big clumps of cash in the river out by the town dump. He could take them all and put them in a few boxes and cover them with newspaper and store them upstairs until next year and they would be fine. They might feel a little grainy and flimsy to the touch but they would be all right. People would buy them because they were there. They would do the trick. They would be better than having no card at all.

The boxes of chocolates, he guessed, he could keep around a few days and see if anybody was fool enough to buy them—you never knew about these people around here sometimes—and then, if he was still sitting on them he could mark them down and get rid of them that way. It wasn't like he had paid an exorbitant amount for them in the first place. He could mark them down almost half and still make a fairly good profit on them that way.

So he was okay with the cards and the chocolates not getting snatched up by this unromantic panic-stricken bunch, but what he was not okay with was the total abundance of roses lined up in a group on his Valentine Day display table. He ordered them for what he thought was a good price too, but if they weren't gone by dinnertime today he was going to take a bath on them for sure. He knew he couldn't mark down roses and have anybody buy them a day or two late. They lost all their significance if they started getting handed out for Valentine's two or three days after the fact. And he was no expert when it came to flowers, but just a few hours ago he'd detected some tiny brown tint beginning to fleck the edges of a few of the packages. You couldn't just tell these things to hold up once the fading and browning got started. It was inevitable. Ray also knew that once one or two of them started down the road to ruin their fellow brethren wouldn't be too far behind.

The bottom line was nobody cared too much what day this was. So what if it was Valentine's Day and proper protocol called for a person to express his or her love to their sweetheart or significant other or mate for life? Big deal here on the poor side of town. Ray, who hardly ever resorted to music to see him through any form of crisis, could suddenly hear Johnny Rivers in his ear, intoning that very song amid all the clatter and hubbub. It was enough to drive him crazy, he thought, and then when "Secret Agent Man" came on in the jukebox in his head he knew he was in big trouble unless something happened to crack the aura of this day and break this wicked spell descending on the town of Sullivan.

Lillian has been hard at it for three hours now, and there didn't seem to her to be any letup in sight. She needed to go to the little girls' room, and she was fixing to pick up her checklane phone and tell somebody in the office to come relieve her. The only problem was there wasn't anybody in the office, so it seemed a little foolish to call up there. Martha was checking three lanes over and Ray was nowhere to be seen. Probably he was out in the parking lot trying to locate that worthless Derrick again. She could see Derrick's sorry butt hiding somewhere dragging on a Newport, which pissed her off the more she thought about it. Damn it, she'd been trapped in here for three hours and going on four now, and she needed to take a smoke too. She wasn't used to this kind of workplace stress, not where she isn't allowed to move or take a second to get her thoughts straight. She's worked in the grocery business most of her life and she's seen snow before, but this is getting ridiculous. She ought to at least have time to tinkle and take a cigarette break. They don't pay her enough to have to work in conditions like this.

Paulette sees how the lines are continuing to get longer and knows all this is not going to come to an end anytime soon. If the people in charge around this store had any sense they could have solved this problem by teaching a few of the folks working here to run a register. That way when something like this snow scare happened or somebody got sick they'd be able to do something about it and not get caught with their pants down like they are down around their knees right now. Paulette mostly didn't like the idea that she wasn't free to walk away from her check lane and start straightening up a display somewhere, not being able to walk back in the produce room and see if that crazy Lee had some fruit he was re-packaging or traying up she could have herself a sample of, or maybe even to where she could take a minute and call her mother on the phone for a little morning chat. Her mother was old and Paulette tried to talk to her once a day, but she really liked to have these conversations while she was at work and getting paid for it. When she got home in the afternoons she preferred watching television to talking on the phone. A lot of times one of her men friends from church would call her up and want to take her out to eat. Otherwise she just had a pot pie or a TV dinner or something quick. She wasn't about to get involved with a whole lot of cooking after working all day. She'd been married once before and gone through all that already, and what good had it done her? The only reward she'd got for her efforts was a husband who spent all his time fooling around and ended up getting himself a stretch in jail because he shot a fellow who objected to him messing around with his wife. That was Oscar, and when Oscar got out of prison after two and a half years he found himself without a wife. He still calls from time to time when he wants something, but Paulette tells him to leave her alone and go find himself some other woman to torment.

It's been about twenty minutes since they called his help up front to help bag, so Bob Howell decides he needs to go up there and see exactly how busy the store is, because he's not real happy at the thought of working all the back stock out by himself and trying to make an order for tomorrow's truck and keeping the bread and milk and eggs full too. Ray Jenkins doesn't pay him enough for this stuff, this working like he's on a chain gang or something. He for certain doesn't want to hear Ray whining later on about things not getting done, because Bob isn't like all the rest of these worthless fuckers around here. He'll tell Ray right off why things didn't get done and how when he calls what little help Bob's got up front for other things it makes it damn near impossible to get anything accomplished. It just ain't gonna happen, bubba, Bob wants to say. He hasn't come out and said just such a thing yet in his three years of being here, but he can tell it's getting close.

It's been that long since Bob lost his job from Publix down in Jacksonville. He had almost eight years in working a head grocery clerk position there. Things had been going pretty smooth most of the time until Gwen started running around on him a little and he had to go upside her head a couple of times. He hadn't done any drinking and drugging for a little while by then, but he got started back and it started to snowball. Things didn't go his way and a whole lot of it wasn't his fault, but Bob knows he's to blame for most of it anyway. He knew better before it got started and he knew better while it was going on. And he had to admit that the company had been more than fair with him. They gave him chance after chance and warning after warning all the way up to when they finally let him go. They even told him if he cleaned himself up and got his act together he could come back and re-apply and maybe he could get back on. He knew better than that, though. He knew he'd never be able to walk that thin of a line he'd get from them, so he just asked them to let him voluntarily quit and to maybe give him a good reference when he tried to get on somewhere else.

His mother had been divorced from the son of a bitch she was married to for eleven years, so he got in touch with her after what had probably been three years or so to see if she knew of any jobs up her way, which was right outside of Sullivan on a little patch of land she'd got from the divorce, since her ex was on drugs and did a stretch in jail before getting out and getting his throat cut in a fight over some damn woman in a bar. She didn't know of any jobs anywhere around, but she was living in a house with a spare bedroom and Bob packed first and was on the way before asking. He and his mother weren't all that close, but he came north anyway, telling her how she was getting old and she needed somebody around to look out for her. Maybe she believed him and maybe she didn't. She didn't come right out and tell him no, so he came and moved in.

He tried a couple of the big chains down the road toward Jackson but he knew during the interviews he didn't really want to go through all those rules and regulations again. He wanted to be somewhere where somebody wasn't breathing down his neck all the time, so he looked around for private stores. He knew grocery work, so that wasn't the problem. He'd first got a job bagging groceries at a mom and pop store when he was going to high school in Dalton, and he was forty-eight now. He needed to find something like that until he could get back on his feet. It took a while for Ray's to come through, but when he got on he thought it would do for a start. He could work and live with his mother and save all that money he would have been spending on rent. He could give his mom a little money every now and then just to keep her from bitching.

Martha is good at keeping a smile on her face and laughing her way through all sorts of things, but after a while it starts to get old for her. She's very good at not letting it show, but inside her is a grating kind of feeling which starts wearing at her with the knowledge that it is mostly on her efforts that the entire business proposition which is Ray's Bargain Foods is managing to stay afloat. She sometimes wonders what would happen if she was to leave and take her talents somewhere else and leave everyone in the store to fend for themselves. She tries not to play up her own self-importance too much, but she suspects the operation would go to pot after not too very long a time. She is not being pompous about this. She knows this for a fact.

This day and all its chaotic events is just a good example. She has watched Lillian and Paulette from the very beginning of this hectic morning and seen how their speed and demeanor haven't changed even one iota from any other day of the week. It is a head-shaking sort of phenomena to her. A person would think that two people who have been around at a place as long as these two women have would know when to put their feet on the accelerator and when to coast, but the sad truth was with Lillian and Paulette it was the same speed, the same behavior, the exact same effort in their jobs every day. Rain or shine, summer, winter, fall, or spring, nothing they did was ever going to be any different. Lillian was going to check at the same pace whether there was one person in line or twenty. She was going to scan three or four items and then stop as if she had to take a breather, gossip a little or say something corny, and then scan another three or four items and do it again. Taking a check or counting back change took all day—it was earth-shatteringly slow. Martha was convinced, after watching such a process for a number of years, that Lillian's pace was a practiced skill, that nobody could truly be this slow without putting great effort into achieving such a result. Martha wondered how many times she had to come out of the office and help Lillian catch up every day, all because Lillian didn't know how or refused to ever shift into high gear.

Paulette was just as bad, perhaps even more so. Paulette could fly on the register when she wanted to; Martha had seen her do it a jillion times. Paulette could turn it on and cut corners and get rid of customers right and left in the blinking of an eye and a good heartbeat, but such actions were never done for good customer service or any endearing quality like that. Paulette only turned it on when she was ready to get out of her check lane and wander off to take a little unscheduled break. Martha could look up and Paulette would be checking, then look down and count some money, then look up again and find Paulette gone, vanished somewhere in the store, down an aisle or to the backroom, leaving one or two customers looking around to see where they should go to pay for their orders, and Martha would have to get up and come out of the office and check them out until Paulette magically appeared from whatever sojourn she'd been on.

It's coming up on ten and Martha still hasn't quite finished her morning bookwork, so she knows she needs to hustle some so the deposit will be ready to go when the Wells Fargo truck comes. For the longest time Ray or Trent just took everything to the bank on their own, but since the shooting at Walgreen's the day after Thanksgiving Ray decided to have an armored car come by and pick the checks and cash up instead. Martha still can't quite get her mind around Ray doing something like this that costs him a little money he could be saving, but she guesses he had a little influence from home on the matter. Probably Betty Jean told her husband he couldn't take chances like that anymore and how the world is a different place than it used to be. People get shot every day over nothing, Martha can hear her say. Just because this is Sullivan doesn't change that one bit.

Speaking of law and order and guns and people maybe getting shot, Martha sees her husband stroll through the door. He is dressed in uniform, so this means he hasn't been home from his overnight shift yet. Probably the snow scare caused a few wrecks and confusion this morning and Pete had to work over. As a policeman, she could never tell about what Pete was into or where he was or when he might get home. Sometimes she wondered if he was actually on the job the entire time he said he was, but she'd learned not to think about that aspect too much. The bottom line was after twenty-odd years of being married to Pete she really didn't care too much anymore. Oh sure, she didn't actually want him running around on her, and, if he was, she certainly didn't want to know anything about it, but as far as it keeping her awake at night worrying over something she couldn't change, well, she'd already moved on from that for a good while now. She hadn't and didn't ever plan to make much of an issue about it, but there it was. She had decided a while back that what was good for the goose was good for the gander too. Of course, to be truthful about the whole situation with Pete, she doesn't really know who was the first to go stepping out—Pete or her. It might have been a tie.

He walks over to the office and looks at her through the glass, and Martha has the usual surge of guilt and fear that Pete is going to immediately accuse her of her wrongdoings. He hasn't ever done anything of this nature yet, but Martha knows he has a temper and there's always a first time for everything.

"I tried to call you this morning, but I couldn't get an answer," he says. "I figured you was in the shower or something. It was about that time."

"I didn't hear my phone," she says. "I may have already been here. I came in a little early because of the snow. I could tell it was going to be busy and I was right." She tried to flash her smile at him like this was a conversation that held some measure of importance, wondering if he was seeing through it or not. "I guess you haven't been home yet either."

"No, I got hung up with the morning shift change. They was all worried about the snow and the morning traffic and they wouldn't let anybody go home until they figured they was on top of it. Town's going to pieces just because they're predicting an inch of snow. Plus it's Valentine's Day. That means somebody's got to shoot somebody or get locked up for domestic assault just to be in keeping with the true meaning of the day."

He looked around at the people and all the chaos on the front end.

"Looks like ya'll are going to have to call for assistance any minute now." He smiles a little like he's just got through cracking a real good joke. "Ya'll are going to have to start firing warning shots over their damn heads just to keep them from trying to steal the fixtures."

"Do you think you'll have to go back in early this afternoon?" she asks. She sees Trent walking in the door now, and she hopes he sees Pete standing here and has sense enough to go to the back office first and talk to Ray before he comes up here. Not that she thinks Pete knows anything about her and Trent, but she'd just as soon Trent keeps his distance anyway. "Do you think they might call you back in if the snow gets too bad?"

"Maybe," he says. He scratches his belly like he is hungry and looks over at the bread rack to see if there are any sweet rolls or doughnuts there. He just finished breakfast but he wouldn't mind nibbling on something else. "How late do you think you'll be working?" he asks. "It's Valentine's Day, you know. If you're lucky I might take you out to eat somewhere before I have to go back in to work. If I don't have to go in too early," he adds, "and you can get off work before the restaurants all close down for the night."

"I hope I can," she says. She sees the customers lining up in Paulette's and Lillian's lines and she's almost glad for the distraction. "Lord," she says. "Look at this. I'm going to have to open up again." She shakes her head and smiles foolishly at him. "I'm having a real hard time getting all my work done this morning.

"I can see that," he says, watching her as she picks up the microphone to call Ray to the office. He's about ready to get out of here. He's got one more stop to make before he goes home. "I would make you ring up some chocolate doughnuts for me," he says, "but it looks like ya'll are out of them. It looks like to me ya'll are about to run out of just about everything."

"It's getting that way," she says as she goes out the office door. Ray hasn't got to the front yet but the people at the window will just have to wait. They've got all day to buy their lottery tickets or pay their electric bill or send Western Unions, so it won't hurt them to stand in line another minute until Ray gets up here.

Trent has heard Martha calling for somebody to come to the front office, but he makes sure he hesitates long enough for Ray to make the trip first. He gets on the computer real quick and acts like he's looking up something important. That way he can sit here for a minute or two extra. He saw Martha's old man standing up front when he came in, and he'd just as soon the fat son of a bitch was gone by the time he goes up there. Trent can do without that kind of drama the first damn thing in the morning. It isn't that he's afraid of Pete Perry or anything like that. He's not. It's just he can do without any unnecessary trouble right now. It took him a while to find this job, and he's not ready to move on to something else just yet. But if any of this ever got out he knows that's exactly what he'll have to do.

Trice Waller is eleven minutes late when he clocks in, which is pretty good for him. It's not too often Trice makes it into work on time, so he doesn't think too much about it when he puts on his apron and takes his time on his way to the front. He doesn't see Mr. Ray anywhere close, so Trice knows all he has to do is slide into the action up front and start bagging for a couple of minutes and act like he's been there all along and not a word will be said—that is, if Mr. Ray hasn't noticed what time it is and is specifically looking for him. Trice doesn't really worry about that either. He knows Mr. Ray isn't going to say anything much, other than the usual "You're late again, Trice. You need to get here on time," and then that will be the end of it. It's not like anybody takes the time to check his time card and see how many times he's been late during the week or gone home early or taken a long lunch. These folks around here have too many other things to worry about. There's never enough help around, and they're just glad to have anybody there no matter what time they show up. Of course they could always hire a few more people, but that might cost a little money, and that cheap ass Mr. Ray ain't about to do anything like that.

Trice has worked for Ray's Bargain Foods off and on for five years now. Mr. Ray has let him go a couple of times in the past, so this is his third go-around. One time he had to do a month in the county pen when he got caught with some weed in a traffic stop, and Mr. Ray got pissed and let him go, then took him back after he got out after he figured Trice had learned his lesson. The second time came when Trice was messing with that Naomi chick and her husband got after him. He'd had to leave town for a few days and lay low a while, so he didn't come to work for a week or so, and Mr. Ray had let him go again. Trice knew he should have called and all that, and he told Mr. Ray how he just wasn't thinking right at the time because somebody was after him with a gun for something he didn't do. It was a case of mistaken identity, he told Mr. Ray, and I was afraid because of that marijuana stuff I was involved in that if I went to the police and told them about it they wouldn't have believed me. So I thought the best thing to do was hide for a few days. I thought if you didn't know where I was then nobody would know where to look for me. I guess I was wrong about that.

Mr. Ray had given him his job back after he thought about it a few days, but he told Trice this was absolutely his last chance.

James sees Trice ease into bagging at Paulette's counter and moves over some to give him room.

"Bout time you got here," he says. "They've had me up here bagging for the last forty-five minutes. These fuckers are about to go crazy around here. I got a pallet of back stock I need to get finished before I leave here today, and I sure as hell ain't going to get it done if I have to stay up here all day."

"Yeah, well I bet you don't mind taking all these tips though, do you? I bet I won't see you turn any of them down when they offer one to you."

"Ain't none of these people going to do no tipping around

here today," James says. "They're too worried about getting snowed in for that. The only time I ever see them tip is Christmas Eve, and that's just in the morning mostly. By the time we get busy in the afternoon nobody even thinks about it."

"I make tips all the time, brother," Trice smiles. "You just don't know how to go about it right, that's all. You have to know how to talk to people. I learned that a long time ago."

"You ain't learned shit," James says. "You just shoot them a line of bullshit so they'll give you some money to make you shut up."

He walks away to help at Ms. Lillian's counter. He doesn't want Mr. Ray to see him and tell him to spread out and not waste time talking.

"You're just jealous because it works," Trice offers him as he leaves. He inches up around the counter so he can be right in back of Paulette. He knows she knows he's back there, but she isn't speaking yet. She's just doing her usual thing of acting like he ain't here and making him speak to her first, like this makes it where she's in control or something. It doesn't bother Trice at all, the way Paulette acts. He sees her do it to every horny brother that comes in the door. There's a bunch of them doing everything they can think of to get in her drawers, and Paulette strings them all out and takes whatever she can get from all of them—meals, rides home to save bus fare, lets them buy her lottery tickets, you name it. She's a trip, man. He's been watching her and trying to get a little action himself for the last couple of years, but he hasn't been successful yet. He doesn't mind that much, though, since he's always got something else on the side somewhere anyway. But he's not going to give up entirely. He's not so sure popping old Paulette would be that great; he's not really sure how old she is. He's thirty-one and he knows she's older than him, but it's hard to tell how much. And it ain't like Paulette gives anybody any clues about it either. She never says where she went to school or how long she's lived in Sullivan or anything like that. Trice thinks she was married once, but she won't even admit to that. She just goes her own way and makes people wonder.

Trent can already tell it's going to be a long day. He's here at work about three hours in advance, but that's not the bad part of it so much. He can take the long hours if he can just pace himself. He doesn't want to be working his ass off every blessed minute he's here, so what he likes to do is take things easy and slow and maybe take a breather here and there to break it up some. He doesn't do this long hours jazz that much anyway, but lets Ray take care of the getting there early and leaving late bullshit. It's his store.

But what he's afraid is going to happen is Ray will get himself all wound up and decide he needs to stay with Trent the whole goddamn night. Trent is worried Ray won't go home at five but keep hanging around finding stuff for everybody—including Trent—to do, and that, what with the snow scare included in the equation, will not be in the least way pretty. Trent has seen Ray act like this before. The Fourth of July always brings it out in him, the parade and the fireworks in the square and the concerts going on down the way by the town hall. Ray acts like anybody who is out and about for the day is going to come in the store and give it a surprise inspection or something, so he darts around from aisle to aisle and from the back to the front like a goddamned irritating horsefly getting on everyone's nerves. He's just as bad on the day before Thanksgiving and Christmas Eve. Maybe it's all holidays. Maybe it's just the least thing different that sets him off. So here there's possibly a snowstorm and here it's Valentine's Day on top of it. There's a hell of a possibility this is a good recipe for disaster.

Trent thinks all this and decides there's no way in hell he's going to get caught up in this shit if he can help it.

From time to time Lyle gets the rail so loaded down he has to stop and let Marcus and Shirley catch up. There's a part of him that wants to tell them to step on the gas a little, but he knows that pretty soon he's not going to have anything more to cut and put out, and all the three of them will be able to do is stand around and look at each other, so at this point there's no need to get in a hurry. He takes this lull as an opportunity to go back to the dock and open the door and see what's happening with the weather. He sees the snow falling fairly heavy, but nothing's sticking just yet. He guesses it's just getting started, that the worst is yet to come.

"Is it doing anything yet?"

Bob Howell has just finished pulling a pallet jack through the doors to get it off the main floor, since it's getting so crowded out there people are having a hard time pushing their carts around it and getting by. After moving it back and forth a few times he's finally given up and pulled it back to the stockroom. He's decided he'll just load up a four-wheeler and do it that way. It'll be easier than moving stuff all the time.

"It's not doing anything but flurrying right now," Lyle observed. "I keep expecting it to start sticking, but so far nothing's happening."

"If it snows enough it's sure going to spoil a lot of people's

Valentine's plans. Nobody will be able to go out to dinner or take a walk in the park or any of that shit." Bob leaned against the alarm bar on the door and observed the falling snow and the lack of accumulation. "Looks to me, though, that right now nobody's got that much to worry about."

"Me and Carol never do any of that stuff on Valentine's day anyway," Lyle said. "There's too many people out and too much of these restaurants jacking up their prices. Course there's not too many restaurants around here anybody would consider fancy enough to go out to on Valentine's Day or something special like that anyway—most people at the church drive in to Jackson and eat at O'Charley's or someplace. We don't do anything like that. We wait until the crowds are all gone and the prices have gone back down until we have our little celebration. Lots of times we'll use a coupon so we can save some money and go somewhere we can find us something for the yard or the house or something like that."

"When I was married I never did anything like that," Bob says.

"That's probably why you're not married anymore," Lyle says. He starts to tell Bob how to have a good marriage a fellow has to work at it each and every day. It doesn't come easily, he wants to say. Lyle is good at this kind of talk, since he's taught the newlyweds' class down at Lowell Street Baptist for fourteen years now. Sometimes—when they have enough couples to make up a class—he can give suggestions and tell stories and make those new brides blush and giggle like it's going out of style. He'll tell those young husbands how they've got to quit worrying about ball games and going to work and mowing the lawn and get themselves inside that house and make sure their better halves are content and happy. He'll tell them about all the bumpy roads he had to travel with Carol before he found the way to balance all his life with the help of God and Jesus Christ. He looks at these couples and tells them how he goes to work and attends church regularly and coaches his Little League baseball team and still has time to take care of his share of the chores around the house and spend quality time with his wife. You have to stay with it every day, he says. You have to put yourself into a partnership with the Lord Jesus Christ and work hard at your marriage night and day, waking and sleeping.

He'd tell Bob all this right now, but he knows it would be just a big waste of breath. Bob Howell doesn't listen to anybody. All Bob Howell is interested in is the Alabama Crimson Tide—even though he's never set foot on the campus—and NASCAR on Sunday afternoons and making sure he's got enough time in the day to go to the front end and watch Martha Perry walk back and forth. Now, granted, Martha's mighty cute for her age and if the truth were known Lyle doesn't mind looking at her sometimes too, but she is a married woman and there's got to be a line drawn somewhere when it comes to things like that. Lyle knows how and when to do it, but Bob Howell doesn't. He just stays up there for the longest time every day getting his eyes full.

"I'm about out of meat to cut," he says finally, just so they both don't stand there in silence watching it try to snow.

"I've got a few more things I can put out," Bob says, "but that's only because that dern fool James doesn't know how to order. It's mainly paper and spices and shit like that, stuff people ain't worrying about having when they get snowed in."

"I don't know. It never surprises me what people start thinking about and worrying about when it starts acting like it's going to snow." Lyle looks at the sky and reaches in his shirt pocket for the pack of Winstons that isn't there anymore. He gave up smoking five years ago, but he still finds himself patting his shirt front for a cigarette every time he stops work or starts thinking about something. He keeps thinking he'll stop his patting and searching one of these days, but it hasn't happened yet. "I've seen them do some real dumb things," he adds.

There's a Buick parked on off down the alley beside a dumpster, and as they stand there an old Trans Am pulls up beside it and a guy gets out. He walks over to the driver's window on the Buick and leans his head inside for a minute. He straightens up and goes back to his car and drives off. In a minute the Buick starts up and drives off too.

"We just saw a drug deal going down," Bob says. "I'd lay my next bonus check on it."

"What makes you think you're going to get a bonus?" Lyle grins. He knows this is a sure way to get Bob started. Might as well have some entertainment around here, he thinks.

"I probably won't," Bob says, "if cheap-ass Ray Jenkins has anything to do with it. The last two or three times I've been in to get my evaluation he acted like I was costing him money out the butt or something. I got my money all right, but I sure had to listen to a lot of pissing and moaning before he handed it over. I had to tell him how he never made no money at all in his goddamn grocery department until I came along. He forgets what sorry shape it was in before I got here."

"Maybe you ought to consider working for free for a while

until Ray can get this place back on its feet." Lyle can see Bob tightening his hands on the dock rail and clenching his jaws. He knows he ought to stop and go back to work, but he likes listening to Bob run his mouth and watching him maybe pop a gasket. He sometimes wonders what prompted Ray to ever hire Bob to begin with. Couldn't he see how finely drawn the guy was? Didn't Ray ever check his references? Didn't he know Bob got fired down in Florida for flying off the handle too much and coming in drunk a time or two too many? Lyle wonders about the way people run their businesses sometimes, but he has taught himself to keep his mouth shut about it. It doesn't say Lyle's Bargain Foods on the sign out front, and that's a good thing too. It means he really doesn't have to worry about anything but the meat department. The rest everybody else can take care of, but not him.

Bob is doing his best not to listen to this damn Lyle too much, because he knows how Lyle just wants to egg something on once he figures out a person has something nagging at them. He's used to the way Lyle is, how Lyle gets his kicks making people mad sometimes and pushing them right up to the brink, doing this while all the time talking up to everybody around him about what a big Christian he was and how he was always busy with the church and doing God's business and all that bullshit. He's concentrating on tuning Lyle out when he hears the crashing sound coming from the side of the building where the parking lot is, so he sticks his head around the corner to see what's happening. There's a big black Chevy pickup sitting with a PT Cruiser attached to the driver's side of it, or at least that's what it looks like. It looks like the Cruiser is growing out of the truck somehow, like the truck's a big plant and the Cruiser is a branch spreading out so it can bloom. Bob can see where the Cruiser has pulled out from a parking spot and rammed into the Chevy as it was coming down the lane looking for a spot to park and come in to shop. In a few seconds he sees the Cruiser's door open and a woman stick her leg out. He doesn't see how anybody could be hurt, but she just sits there with her leg hanging out and the driver of the truck doesn't move or anything. Bob can't tell who it is because the windshield is tinted a real dark gray and he can't make out who's in there.

"They're trying to kill each other out in the lot," he tells Lyle.

Lyle looks around at the two vehicles for a minute and then goes back inside. He decides to go back to the meat department and cut some more meat for a while. That way he won't have to get involved as a witness or anything. He's got better things to do than talk to insurance adjusters or get called in to testify in court.

Bob knows he ought to go back inside too, but he has to wait and see what happens when the two drivers finally get out and start talking to each other. Maybe there will be a fight, which he'd hate like hell to miss. He's seen some people duke it out in the parking lot before, and it's been pretty good entertainment. It might be even better if the truck's driver is a woman too. Some of these small town girls can get right sometimes. Some of them have bad tempers and can get set off pretty quick. He'd really hate to miss that if it was to happen. So he decides to be patient and wait and see what goes down.

The driver of the truck is a redneck named Cliff who Bob knows from hanging out at the Stardust the three or four nights a week Bob goes there for a sandwich and a couple four beers or so. Cliff likes to sit at the end of the bar and watch football games on the overhead TV and drink a Miller Lite for each quarter and one for the road after the game ends. He's not a bad guy—works for a little electric company downtown someplace. Bob's talked to him a few times about Alabama, since Cliff wears a Tide hat around all the time. He's okay as far as it goes. Bob is sorry to see his new Silverado's been wrecked.

"Damn, Lyle," Bob said, "take a look at this."

He looked back inside so he could motion to Lyle and point out to him just exactly what kind of craziness was going on in their parking lot, but Lyle has gone back to his meat department already and Bob is alone at the back door to watch the mayhem unfolding before him all by himself.

The woman in the PT Cruiser has gotten out of her smashed vehicle and thrown down her cigarette at Cliff the electrician's work boots. She is shaking her finger and raising her not very lady-like language up in decibels enough so that Bob, who is a good long Crimson Tide field goal away from the two, has no trouble hearing or deciphering exactly what is on that woman's mind. She tells Cliff he is a sorry asshole and a menace to society. She screeches out to him how she is going to make sure he is fired from his job and how maybe she'll see he does a little time in the workhouse too. She is in a hurry, she tells him, and he could have waited a few seconds for her to pull out of her slot and be on her way.

About this time her phone chirps out some ring tone with Miranda Lambert leading the way, and the woman stops in her disgust and indignation toward Cliff to answer her cell and recount to whoever is on the other end how Cliff the electrician had come along out of nowhere and placed his truck right in her way. No, Bob hears her say, it looks like I ain't going to get to go bowling this afternoon either.

She hangs up her phone and is approaching Cliff with her fists all balled up and threatening to get her gun out of the glove box and shoot his fucking ass if he doesn't get his truck moved away from her car within about ten seconds when the police car pulls up behind the truck and parks there with his blue light going around in a circle. Bob is all set to see if the officer, whose name Bob doesn't know but is a guy who came in the store about every morning to buy cigarettes and Vienna Sausages, gives the woman a ticket, and, if she does, if she will go off on the officer and maybe get arrested or something good like that. Bob even thinks with as wild as she is carrying on some pepper spray or maybe even a Taser might be in order, and he would sure hate to miss that. He is intent to watch until the conclusion of the show until he sees the backroom door swing open and Ray come walking through, going about a hundred miles an hour like his butt is on fire.

"We don't have time for smoke breaks this morning, Bob. We're up to our ears out there right now. Soon as you can you need to fill up the milk and eggs again. Ten more minutes and they're both going to be empty."

"I just had James fill them up about an hour ago." He shuts the back door and latches it. His face is turning red like it always did when Ray gets on him for something. "He must have done his usual half-ass job on them, about like always."

Ray doesn't say anything, but just continues toward the back office like there was a fire blazing down the steps and he had to save somebody more important than Bob from the flames. Bob watches him go and feels his usual familiar feeling of fear and anger in his head, fear of the thought of getting fired again and having to go through the process of looking for a job at his age, and anger that he was in such a position where he had to every day watch his back and not step on any toes so he can maintain a place to come to five times a week and make a buck. He is forty-six years old; it is a pile of shit to have to live like this from day to day and week to week.

The snow everyone was waiting on began falling in hesitant patterns. For a moment the air would be white and visibility would seem to be slipping away, but then, just as soon as the town was convinced the storm was at last here in earnest, the precipitation would suddenly let up and abate and slink away into nothing. The sky would grow darker and clouds would gather, convincing everyone the storm was reloading and would come again soon and this time not go away. So, the weather seemed to be saying, you'd better get ready. It won't be long. You better pay attention to what is happening.

Lee has had about enough of this bagging business and is ready for a breather. It's been almost three hours now since he got in, and he hasn't had one single minute to relax. His head is still aching from last night, and he knows about the only way he's going to feel any better is when he's had a chance to drink a Pepsi from the machine in the back and maybe nod off in the produce cooler for about a half an hour. He's got to where this is pretty much a normal part of his work day. He gets his Pepsi and a bag of salted peanuts and goes back to the cooler. He slides a four wheeler in with him and sets two boxes on it—juice, salad dressing, something like that—and then he sits down on the boxes of back stock lettuce stacked against the wall and eats his peanuts and takes a few swigs of Pepsi. Usually he'll sneak a cigarette while he's sitting there, and maybe he'll even do a little number if he is able to buy some off of Derrick that morning. He's got a little pimento jar that he's emptied where he can squelch his butts and roaches so they're hidden away and not on the cooler floor, so that's covered in case his dad or somebody starts snooping around back there. When he's had his peanuts and his Pepsi and his cigarette or dooby he can semi-close the door and sit on the lettuce boxes and lean back against the wall and close his eyes for a few minutes. If he hears somebody coming or if they open the door he can stand up really fast and act like he's loading the four wheeler with stock so he can get back on the floor and make the department look good. All this is a lot of trouble to go to just for a few minutes worth of relaxation, and he'd just as soon sneak out the back door and go home, but he knows he can't get away with that for a while. His dad has been keeping an eagle eye on him lately.

The big problem is he can't seem to sneak away because he knows he's going to be missed if he does, even though Derrick and Trice and Larry are all up here bagging. Trent has come up and opened up the fourth register now, and every time Lee looks up he sees he's about the only bagger up front. Derrick and Trice are outside and nowhere to be found, and that damn Larry is hustling every order he can out the door, meaning he's either trying to get a bunch of tips or he's got that fear in his head again that if he doesn't bust his ass every second he's here at work Lee's dad is going to fire him. Lee has started to tell Larry to slow his butt down a lot of times, to stop worrying about losing his job because Lee's dad isn't about to let him go, but there's something in Lee's head that keeps him from telling Larry to ease up, because, if he does, it just means there's more work left to do for somebody, and Lee is afraid that somebody just might be him. So he keeps his mouth shut for now.

Nobody has had a break so far, and Ray knows Lillian and Paulette are fixing to start in bitching about it pretty soon, so he starts thinking about how he's going to relieve them. The lines are too long to just close them off with the chains at the end of the lanes that stretch across and keep customers from piling up their items on the conveyor belts, and he can't wade through the crowd and try to block either of them off with a merchandise display, because there's just too damn much traffic to reach them. It's getting close to noon and he wonders if the schools have dismissed early by now, but Martha is out in a register again, so he can't run to the back and turn the TV on to see what's happening. He keeps trying to get some of his afternoon school kids on the phone but nobody is answering. He wonders if they're all still in class or if they're just ignoring his call because they don't want to come to work.

Nobody has bought any flowers. There's still a whole table of candy and cards. It's like Valentine's Day doesn't even exist this year.

Trent has jumped in a checklane after waiting a few strategic minutes for Martha's old man to leave. He's gone ahead and started checking even before Ray had the chance to tell him to, so at least he's not bristling from being ordered around right off the bat when he gets here. But he's damned if he's going to stay in this register and check out these hordes of panicky people the whole goddamn day. No, he'll whittle this crowd out and get some of the part-time kids in here as quick as he can. He'll get on the phone and call the school office and make them take messages to them while they're sitting in class. He's done this a couple of times before, and it's never failed to get a couple of the money-hungriest of the crew to come on in as fast as they can.

They'll do it for me, Trent thinks, especially the girls. I can get a couple of the girls to do anything I want. Sometimes he has to keep his imagination from running too wild. This is the only job he has right now, you know.

Martha watches Trent checking out of the corner of her eye. She is in the stand next to him, and when she steps out to get a flyer from the office window to check a price she can almost reach over and touch him. She thinks about how they were touching each other last night. They've gone to bed with each other at least ten times now, but last night was the first time they'd actually slept together all night. She doesn't know what she thinks about that. When she woke up after a while she had just laid there feeling afraid. She didn't know what would happen if the two of them ever got caught. Pete had such a bad temper. And she had to admit it—she didn't much like taking such a big chance. Playing around with Trent was fine as long as it didn't get too involved. She liked to keep things short and sweet that way. She hadn't really given a whole lot of thought to what might happen if their meetings didn't start and end during its appointed time. She didn't much care for this feeling she had right now of not really being in control. She was going to have to watch it and be more careful. Trent was okay, but it wasn't like this was any big love affair. She wasn't going to kid herself about that.

Mrs. Moseley appeared through the front door again, looking around for a spare bascart so she could fill it up one more time. Martha guessed the hundred dollars she'd spent two hours ago hadn't quite depleted her EBT card yet, so she was back to finish the job.

"I just heard the noon news!" she told everyone. "It's coming down in Memphis right now! It's coming, it's on the way." She looked around to make sure everyone was listening. "It won't be long now," she said.

FIVE
1:00 P.M.

Not an inch of snow has fallen, but there's no bread left on the rack except for some raisin bread that went out of date two days ago. Ray starts to call two of the local bread companies to see if he can get some more product in, but he knows it's useless to try this late in the day, since most of the route men have already come back in and are on their way home by now. These guys start work at four in the morning, so by this time of day it's all over.

The snow is falling but not sticking. Ray doesn't know if it's because the front hasn't moved through and it's still too warm to accumulate or exactly what the meteorologists on all the stations are predicting right now, because he's stuck on the front end and can't get time enough to get back to his office so he can see what the television reports are saying. All he can rely on right now is hearsay from the customers, and who knows how accurate any of that is? From his experience in retail grocery he's learned that people will say just about anything just to hear the sound of their own voices, and it doesn't matter if it's true or not.

The chocolates and the flowers on the table are still there.

A young guy who might be eighteen walks up to the office window. Ray has never seen him before, and he immediately wonders if he's skipping school or something, since he doesn't look old enough to him to be walking around and not be required to be sitting in school at this time of day. But maybe schools have let out by now—how would Ray know, being stuck up in the office like this and not privy to any outside communication with the world or anything? The boy fishes some paper out of his pocket and takes out his billfold. He unfolds the paper and holds it up for Ray to see.

"I'd like to see if I can cash my paycheck," he says. He is smiling and is oh so polite, both of which look utterly fake to Ray. Anytime he sees these two actions in tandem together he grows immediately wary and altogether suspicious.

"I'll have to take a look at it," he tells the boy. Despite the big grin on his face, there is something about this kid Ray doesn't like. Ray has been around long enough to know when somebody is up to something.

The check is a personal one, written on the account of Jim and Janet Odle from one of the local Sullivan banks. Ray looks at the amount of five hundred dollars written in and the notation "Roof Work" inserted in the description column. He looks at this kid, who may be seventeen at the most, and tries to imagine him up on somebody's roof doing repairs. He also looks at Jim Odle's signature on the front and notices how it looks similar to the signed name on the back, Barry Mangrum.

"What kind of roofing work did you do for Mr. Odle?" he asks.

"I replaced a few shingles," Barry Mangrum says. "There were a few places leaking, so I took care of that too."

"We've got some leaks in our roof," Ray says. "Maybe I ought to talk to you about getting them fixed."

Ray is looking at the drivers license for Barry Mangrum, and it's about as fake as he's ever seen. Somehow or another it's an altered license that's been fixed and altered and then copied off on some color printer, then stuck inside some laminated piece so you couldn't tell how cheap the paper was by the touch. The picture is not even whoever this Barry Mangrum character is; it's some fellow who's at least fifteen years older and has ears that stick out like Dumbo the elephant. Ray has seen some stupid imitations and attempts at forgery in his time, but this one takes the cake.

"It looks like you've changed a little since this picture was taken," he smiles. He sees Trent taking notice of what is transpiring and moving behind the boy, but Ray doesn't try to let on that anything is happening in the background. He keeps smiling and fingering the check and the fake i.d. "You're awfully young to be such a professional in the roof business, and if I was a betting man I'd say this picture isn't you at all. So how about I call this number on the check and see if this fellow really wants to advance you this much money for working on his roof?"

The kid knows the jig is up and starts to bolt and make a beeline for the door. He doesn't realize Trent is behind him and looks surprised when he gets grabbed around the shoulders. But Trent is not the strongest and most burly person in the store this minute, and the boy twists and turns and is finally successful in breaking free. He runs for the door and Trent takes about two steps before he lets up and slows down. Whatever this kid is up to, Trent tells himself, it's not worth getting all that involved in. It's fine to make a show of it like he's trying to do something to impede the kid's escape—whatever might look good to Ray—but it's another when it comes to maybe getting hurt or injured or anything like that. What if this kid is armed? People carry guns these days, all the fucking time. He is not ready to take a bullet for the sake of Ray's Bargain Foods, so he makes certain he's moving slow enough that molasses could beat him to the door.

Larry is the only one who makes a move to stop him, and it's an impressive move at that, a hard-driving tackle at the door directly in the kid's chest that carries them both into the bread rack and sends them as a duo bouncing off into the floor. Trent watches the action and is impressed with the takedown. He's seen players on the Tennessee Titans who could take a few lessons from Larry. Trent reminds himself to always be kind and polite to Larry from here on out, to be a nice guy and stay on Larry's better side. He needs to make sure he doesn't ever do anything to piss Larry off.

Since the bread rack is essentially empty all that comes down on impact is most of the wire rack that stretches across the front end, which collapses in a heap like it has been dynamited and falls upon Larry and the potential forger as they struggle on the floor. Larry is too much for the younger and lighter boy and soon has him in a headlock while lying on top of him and pinning him to the tile.

"Stop trying to get away or I'm going to twist your damn head off," Larry tells him. Trent watches all this going on and sees no reason to doubt that Larry could probably do exactly what he is saying.

Ray runs out from the office and gets all the way to where the two men are sprawled on the floor. He stops for a minute and considers whether he ought to go and get his pistol out of the top of the safe, but it looks to him like Larry has control of the situation and can keep the kid pinned until the police get here. Ray has called them just before he came out to help, but he doesn't have any idea how long it will take them to get there. He hopes it's not too long. It's not like the streets are icy and snowy and filled up with people slipping and sliding and running into each other or anything. He'd like to get this all taken care of before it scares off the business and people go and shop somewhere else. He looks around at the long lines and every cashier checking as fast as they can, the customers and his employees so involved in each of their own personal dramas that they can scarcely take the time to view this physical battle going on ten feet in front of them. It appears to Ray that everyone has determined there aren't any firearms present in the situation, so nobody is going to get shot and perhaps die in their quest for bread and milk and toilet paper.

Luckily, the policeman who'd been outside giving a ticket to the woman in the PT Cruiser who slammed into Cliff's new pickup has come inside to get a pack of cigarettes, so he walks right up on the two men writhing and contorting on the floor with half the bread rack on top of them. Ray walks over and hands the alleged forged check to the officer and points down at the two tangled bodies on the floor.

"The white guy on the bottom is the one who had the check," he tells the officer. "The fellow on top is one of my employees."

"Looks like he might deserve a raise," the officer, whose name is Jimmy Parsons, says. "Looks like he's gone above and beyond the call of duty."

Jimmy cracks a small smile and chuckles a little. He likes to intersperse a little of his wit when he's on the job. He likes for people to think of him as a cool customer who doesn't get all flustered and caught up with the action. He's going to move to a big city and be a detective one day, after he gets a few years experience. He can see his style play out real good in a position like that. He'd be like one of those guys he sees on television.

Larry gets off the suspect and he and Jimmy pull him up and march him to the back office while everybody continues to stand in line and gawk while waiting to get checked out. Nobody's worried about getting shot or if somebody is going to jail or not. All they're doing is waiting and squinting their eyes to see out the window by the front doors, wondering if it's started snowing for real or not yet.

Derrick isn't going anywhere near Larry and this dude on the floor. He doesn't really know what is going on yet, but he's been around this store and this neighborhood long enough to know that when some kind of scuffle like this gets started it's best to give it a wide clearance until you figure out if somebody's going to come up with a piece or not. These days dudes and crazy-ass chicks go packing a lot more than they used to—you just never know who's got what concealed somewhere. Derrick's got a little heat he carries around himself, but he doesn't bring it to work much. Sometimes he thinks he ought to because of shit like what is going on now on the floor in front of him, but he knows if Mr. Ray got wind of him carrying while he was on the clock there'd be a lot of trouble coming from it. He might even get fired for it, although Derrick doubts Mr. Ray would ever go that far. Derrick knows Mr. Ray would have a hard time finding somebody who'll stick around and work as cheap as he has for Mr. Ray these past eight years. And there's also the fact that Mr. Ray doesn't like to fire people much—like hardly ever. Mr. Ray's got a problem when it comes to letting people go. Sometimes he lets people get away with a whole lot. Derrick thinks of a few times he's got away with some stuff too.

Lillian doesn't say anything about it to anybody, but she knows who this boy is that they're taking to the back office. He's the youngest son of Lila Holt, who is a regular customer here at the store and always likes to come through Lillian's line so they can gossip and share stories with each other. Lillian doesn't really like Lila all that much, but Lila brings her cookies from time to time and sometimes they both stand out on the sidewalk and smoke cigarettes together. Lillian is like this with a lot of her customers. She likes to be friendly and appear to be on intimate relationships socially with a good percentage of them, since this way it appears to Ray and Trent and Martha and everybody else in the store that she is connected to many people who are the lifeblood of the company, and if something were to happen to her then these people would all stop shopping here and the store would close. Lillian likes to feel like she holds a lot of cards and has power, so no one at the store –she thinks—wants to mess with her. She feels as long as she has these aces in the hole in her possession Ray and all the rest will continue to suck up to her and handle her with kid gloves, since she is so important to the welfare of the business. Lillian likes feeling like she is the queen of this environment, and every day and every decision that goes on at Ray's Bargain Foods transpires with her in mind.

She doesn't know what Lila's son has done, but she'll find

out and see if she can sway anything too bad from happening to him. She'll tell Ray who the boy's mother is and how she's a real good customer who spends a lot of money here. Ray is hungry for business so much he'll probably listen to her and take her advice, and Lila on the other hand will be grateful. It will be a win-win situation for her either way. Lillian likes the way it sounds. She likes people owing her favors.

Paulette knows the boy too. She's seen him come in with his mother back when he was little, and she didn't much care for him back then either. If you ask her, he was a spoiled little white boy then, and it looks like not much has changed, even if he is maybe ten years older. Paulette hasn't seen this boy in a while, but she remembers his face and she remembers him just fine. She caught him once when he was eight or so, stealing a candy bar off one of the merchandisers when he thought nobody was looking. Paulette had seen him, though. She'd come up on him as he was trying to stuff it down in his pocket and made him put it back. She'd told him then that if he ever did anything like that again she'd tell his mother. She'd started to do it then anyway, just because she didn't like Mrs. Lila that much. She didn't like any of these people who were all the time sucking up to Lillian. She'd let him go, though, even if he was Mrs. Lila's kid, mainly because she didn't want to fool with either one of them. Now here he was doing something else. She was glad he got caught—whatever it was. Some people never learned a lesson. That was the truth.

Trice is just coming back in the door after an extended stay outside, so he only catches the last of what's just happened on the front end. He sees the cop and Larry and Mr. Ray going toward the back with the white dude and he wonders if anybody has noticed how he wasn't around when everything was going down. It makes him a little nervous to think about it, on account he was selling a little weed to a guy right around the corner and the cop that was out on the other side giving a ticket got through pretty quickly and then walked up and went inside the store without Trice seeing him. Goddamn, Trice thinks, I must be slipping or something. I need to be paying attention a whole hell of a lot better than that.

Trice starts bagging for Paulette again but he can't shake the thought out of his mind. He's always prided himself on being smart and careful, and here he is not even an hour into his work shift and he's letting some cracker cop almost walk up and catch him selling red-handed. He has got to be more careful than this, that's for sure. The word is already out that there's a guy coming after him for messing around with some girl Trice doesn't even remember. Supposedly, Trice keeps hearing, he's not only screwed this dude's girlfriend but he shorted him out in some deal back a few months ago. This is all news to Trice. He can't put a face on some whore he's supposed to have fucked, and he for damn sure can't remember every single brother he's sold to. He doesn't even believe any of it is true. He doesn't know anybody who's that tied up to any woman, and everybody knows he's a square shooter on the marketplace. Sometimes rumors and shit just get started because motherfuckers like to talk.

Maybe there is a little bit of trepidation in the air, because suddenly the checkouts thin down and the front is semi-deserted for a moment. Martha wonders if the big rush is over and the customers are gone for good, or if the weather forecasters have changed their predictions and called off the snow, or if the appearance of a policeman and a restrained man after a struggle has made everyone back off for a little while and not want to be in the mix when shots are fired or violence is rendered. She's pretty sure it's the last choice. She knows these people. They're not through panicking over the coming snow by a long shot. There's a lot more left to go before anybody around this store can say they've made it safely through the day.

It's half past one and she's so far behind it's not funny. She's got to figure out how to get Lillian and Paulette out of their lanes for lunch. She needs more help in here, like a half hour ago she needs them. She can't just close a lane and let the customers line up to Timbuktu. Plus, she's got her own work she has to get done. She hasn't finished getting the deposit done yet. The armored car is going to be here any minute. They're running late or they'd have been here already.

"When is the earliest we can get some of these school kids in here?" She stands behind Trent, who is checking at what for him is a fast rate, and poses the $64,000 question. For a moment she starts to put her hands on his hips but decides not to. She wonders if she might distract him and slow him down. There's a time and place for everything, Martha, she tells herself. You need to concentrate on what's going on here at work.

"I've got calls in to all of them," he says over his shoulder. "I haven't heard back from anybody yet. Regular school isn't out until three though. I was hoping they'd dismiss early because of the snow, but I don't think that's going to happen."

"Well, it's not snowing yet," she says, "so I guess you can forget that part of the plan."

Ray and Larry are still in the back with the policeman and the guy Ray caught doing something—Martha doesn't know what kind of crime has been attempted that's caused such a ruckus—but she decides she is just going to go ahead and do what she needs to do without asking Ray and having him hem-hawing around and acting like somebody has stuck a knife in him. She has to get something going now and she can't wait around for somebody else to do anything to solve the problems.

She walks back to the meat department and goes through the doors to the prep room. Lyle is looking over his order catalogue and Marcus and Shirley are looking out the one-way glass at all the people buying out their rack. Lyle looks up at Martha and smiles, while Shirley and Marcus wonder why she's come back to where they work. It's not like she does this all the time. Now that they think about it, they can't remember her ever coming back here, so something must be up.

"Did you get tired of working up front?" Lyle asks. "I'd put you to work back here, but right now there's nothing for you to do. We've already put everything in the cooler out. Once they buy all that there's nothing more that we can do."

"That's why I'm here," Martha smiles. "I knew you were just the kind of fellow to help me out in my time of trouble." Martha flashes her sweetest smile and giggles like she's some flirty schoolgirl. She knows how Lyle is and thinks this is probably the best way to get what she wants without there being a big fight or show about it. "I thought if you had everything done back here you might consider letting me use Shirley and Marcus up front for a while."

"I was just fixing to send them home."

"Well, what I was thinking was I'd bring everybody up front so I can get Lillian and Paulette out for lunch. They've been checking the entire morning and haven't even had time to even go to the restroom."

"I don't know how to check," says Marcus.

"You won't have to," Martha smiles at him. "I'll just use you as a bagger and let Trice go in behind Lillian. Then I'll use you," she says to Shirley, "to relieve Paulette and let her go home. Maybe by the time we get all the breaks and lunches out of the way the school kids will come in and we'll finally have enough help to operate."

"I don't know if I remember how to check anymore," Shirley says. "I haven't been on a cash register in a while."

"It's been three months," Martha says. "I gave you a quick lesson right before Thanksgiving, remember? Anyway, these registers are easy. They almost do everything for you where you don't even have to know anything. And somebody will be right there if you have any questions. I'm not going anywhere, I promise. All you have to do is holler at me and I'll come right down. I won't let you drown."

Martha can tell this arrangement doesn't set too well with Lyle, but she takes Marcus and Shirley with her quickly before he has the opportunity to protest. She already knows he's going to go to Ray and protest about how the hours she uses Shirley and Marcus on the front end are going to get skewed and charged to him and come off his meat department's bottom line, which is going to affect his bonus in April, but Martha already has an answer for that. She makes Shirley and Marcus fill out two new time cards and label them Front End, and while she's at it she gets one for Larry and Lee too. She laughs to herself at all this childish preparation. But she's not going to have Lyle and Bob acting like they're getting messed with or shorted. They are both like two little boys who she has to outthink before they have the chance to act up. She wouldn't let one of them think the other was getting treated better than the other. And as for Lee, she might as well include him in the big picture too. Ray wouldn't care so much about how he was getting used, but there was no sense in not grouping him in right with the others. That way they could all feel like they were in the same boat and nobody was getting treated any differently than anybody else.

In the back office Ray stands by his desk while the policeman writes his report. Larry stands by the door and watches the forger dude sit in a chair and lean to one side, like he's fixing to fall asleep and tumble out of the chair. Larry is about calmed down now; he's not nervous and twitchy like he was when they first got down here. He supposes he had a lot of adrenaline going from wrestling around on the floor up front, but he thinks that doesn't have all that much to do with it. What it is for him is the fact he doesn't like to be anywhere where a cop is, and here he is in this little room in the back with this policeman sitting two feet away from him. He's pretty sure the guy is going to look over at him any minute and say something like "Haven't I seen you somewhere before?" Larry is afraid maybe it's true and the guy has, even though he himself doesn't remember this cop at all. But he's been around a few cops the last couple of years. This guy might very well know him from one of those times. It's not like Larry has done anything too bad lately he needs to feel nervous about, but he hasn't been totally innocent all the time either. Like, for example, the pot he's got rolled up in his sock right now. He doesn't like being around somebody like this who may just decide to run him in too just for fun. Larry is just glad the dude hasn't got a dog with him. A damn dog would sniff him out in a second. Of course, this ain't that big of a town. Larry's not even sure the police even have a dog on their force. They probably can't afford it.

Supposedly this forger dude is handcuffed to the arm of the chair he's sitting in, but all of a sudden the guy has managed to work one end of the cuffs off the end of the arm and free himself to where he can stand up quick and bolt for the door before Larry has a chance to snap to attention and make a grab for him. He pushes Larry back against the wall and takes off down the hallway running, then he's up the stairs and heading through the stockroom for the door that leads out to the main floor and on up front to the checkouts and the front door and the parking lot. Jimmy the policeman jumps up from behind the desk and takes off down the hallway behind Larry, who is already in pursuit, leaving Ray sitting alone in his office wondering if he should get up and join in on the chase too. For a moment he tries to remember whether Jimmy the policeman ever searched the forger to see if he was armed, and when he remembers that he did and the guy had nothing on him, Ray gets up and takes off down the hallway too. He's okay doing this as long as there's no chance he's going to get shot or stabbed or anything like that.

From his checklane where he's been marooned more than an hour now, Trent sees the fellow who's just been detained suddenly unencumbered and making his way up the second aisle in a weave like he's a border collie in an agility contest, in and out of people and bascarts jammed together who inch together and try to get out of the way as the forger and Larry and Jimmy the policeman and Ray bringing up the rear pass through as fast as they can negotiate. Elbows are brushed and boxes of Uncle Ben's Rice and Delmonico Spaghetti get knocked off the shelf and fall in the floor. Ray tells everybody how sorry he is as he brings up the rear.

The fugitive is headed Trent's way and Trent has to make the decision if he's going to leave his checklane and try and stop him again or stay where he is with his head down checking and scanning and act like he doesn't see the guy coming his way or any of this action going on around him whatsoever. Maybe Derrick or Trice will jump in there, he thinks, but he knows better than that. He sees Martha leading Shirley and Marcus to the front from the meat department, so maybe Marcus will do something. Trent doesn't know. All he's worrying about is whether he should get involved or not. He didn't come in to work early today so he could possibly get hurt or maimed. Like a lot of duties around Ray's Bargain Foods, Trent is hopeful somebody else will jump in and do it before he is forced to himself.

The forger is fast on his feet and nimble as all getout, so keeping up with his gait, much less catching him, is more than enough for Larry and Jimmy the policeman to accomplish. Before he became a meth user, Ronnie--who is not really a Barry--the forger/thief/fugitive had once been on the track team down in Lawrenceburg when he was a sophomore, before he dropped out and left town after he got placed on probation for a year for possession of a bag of weed. He was smart enough to wait until his probation was up before he left, but he still up and took off without telling his mother he was going, so she doesn't know where he is right now. His dad's been gone a long time so that doesn't matter. He's called his mother once about three weeks ago but he wouldn't tell her where he was. He just said he'd be home sooner or later. Now he knows if he gets caught it's going to be a whole lot later and not one bit sooner. He doesn't like thinking about the possibilities right now.

He runs in between a black woman holding a baby and a white woman waiting to get a carton of cigarettes at the office, who has just stepped away from the window to ask Trent to go get her Bel-Airs for her because there's nobody up there right now. Ronnie tries to avoid running into the black woman and the baby and instead plows into the white woman wanting cigarettes, and the two of them stumble over into a guy pushing a bascart, and they all three go hurtling into a Pepsi display where a stack of twelve packs and a couple of rows of two liters collapse and start rolling and spewing on the floor. People begin moving and jumping out of the way to not be in the middle of the chaotic fight or have carbonated Pepsi spray on them.

Larry almost has his hands on Ronnie, but Ronnie breaks free and skirts around Paulette's checklane for the door. He thinks he has a clear shot until a woman walks by on the outside and the electric door doesn't open and Ronnie ends up smashing up against the glass like a bug on a windshield, splattered there long enough for Larry to gain another two steps on him and get close enough to try and grab him again. Ronnie regains his balance and jumps the small stanchion between the In and Out doors and shoulders his way out the In door to the lot. He has his mom's old car he took off in parked at the other side of the building but he doesn't head that way right now with Larry and Jimmy and Ray all pretty close behind him, so he runs instead toward the street hoping he can get across and go lose himself behind the houses where there are woods and undeveloped land he can use to put some distance between himself and this posse that is trying to overtake him. He can run like the wind when he wants to, so he believes if he can just get to a point where he can stretch his legs and get to full speed there's no way any of his pursuers will be able to catch him.

It's a good idea except for the cars lined up on the upgrade trying to get to places and work and home before the snow gets here, so Ronnie tries to dart in between two stationary cars and cross over right at the time the driver of a motorcycle behind the two stalled ones gets impatient and pulls out quick and tears out up the turning lane to make a left and take a shortcut over the hill to avoid this confusion. He's just through winding into third gear when Ronnie steps out and the front wheel and fender smack into him and sends him flying across the hood of a car while the bike's wheel turns hard left and scoots over into the opposite lane of traffic. The sound of screeching brakes makes everyone stop trying to check out and causes a few to run to the door and look and see if anybody got killed or not.

While he's sprawled on the pavement and harboring thoughts of maybe dying, Ronnie thinks about how this is Valentine's Day and if he was still back in his old home town and hadn't gotten himself arrested he could still maybe be the boyfriend of Betsy Farmer, who he thought had liked him enough to maybe put out a little if he'd tried. But that was all over now, he thought, since he was probably dying here in the middle of the road and at least maimed for life with all sorts of bones in his body broken and twisted. He didn't need to be worrying about how he should have done things different so he wouldn't be in the state he was in right now, because the fact of the matter is he most definitely is in this state and there's no getting around it and no amount of praying about it or crying about it is going to change the fact that here he is right now and he's all fucked up and things don't look like they're ever going to get any better.

Larry is the first to arrive, but he doesn't jump on Ronnie AKA Barry Mangrum this time because the way Ronnie's all decked out there it's pretty obvious he's not going anywhere anytime soon. Jimmy makes it to the scene about a minute later, puffing and gasping for air like this is the hardest thing he's ever had to do and he for damned sure didn't have to do anything this strenuous to have to qualify to be a cop here in Sullivan. Ray is still on the other side of the road watching what transpires. He's not so sure he wants to get out in the traffic and get hit, and he's also sure he doesn't want to get involved in any more wrestling or violence or maybe even having to witness a death. No sir, he can see just fine from where he is. He doesn't have to step right back into the fray of the action just this very minute. He didn't get into the grocery business so some nut can shoot him or put him in a position where he gets splattered by oncoming traffic or get his body marred by wrestling vicious criminals. No, there's enough he has to put up with other than this. There is a limit, whether his wife or his employees or his customers think there is or not.

With Mr. Ray out in the street and Mrs. Martha busy teaching Shirley to remember how to check and Trent in a checklane, Trice thinks it's a good time to go to the back and take an unscheduled break for a few minutes. He goes upstairs to hide in the break room for a while—which is not really a room at all but is just a space carved out among the insulation pipes and the ancient wired merchandisers and the boxes of holiday decorations that date back to the sixties, rotting away and missing pieces and harboring spider eggs wherever somebody hasn't brushed them off in the last decade or so—but he finds he isn't alone when he gets to the top of the steps. Lee stands over by the mini refrigerator grinning at him. He's got the door opened up and is rummaging around to see if he can find anything to eat in there, finally settling on a cold wiener that Trice wouldn't touch with a ten foot pole, since he knows it's been floundering around on the shelf inside there for at least a good month now. He knows it doesn't matter to this damn Lee though. Lee will eat anything, the crazy-ass mother.

"I ain't had a break all morning," Lee says. "Fuck all that crap up there."

"You got a goddamned break when you got hired, asshole, and that was only because your mom screwed up and didn't get you aborted when she had the chance."

Lee grins like this is the funniest thing he's ever heard. Trice decides for about the thousandth time Lee is the goofiest cracker on the face of the earth. The only thing he's not sure of is whether Lee was born this way or if he's just added so many drugs to his system he's fallen off the edge of the earth.

"How come you didn't help your daddy catch that guy up front?" Trice asks, just to see what kind of an answer he gets. This ought to be good, he thinks.

"Shit, I know better than that." Lee has finished his wiener and is looking at a package of sweet rolls that have been in the refrigerator since before Christmas. "That guy could have had a gun on him or a knife or something like that. I wasn't about to fuck with him. Ain't nothing around here all that important to me that I'm going to get hurt over it."

"You mean even if your dear old dad was in big trouble and in danger of losing his life you weren't going to lift a finger to help him?" Trice lights up a cigarette even though he's inside and it's against the rules. He shakes his head and grins at Lee. "What kind of son are you, boy? You ought to be more than willing to lay down your life for your father and this store after all he's done for you. Shit, your daddy done give you a job and looked after your ass and kept you out of jail, and this is the thanks you give him. You're about a worthless honky, ain't you?"

Lee keeps smiling while he sniffs a sweet roll and stuffs it into his mouth.

"May be worthless," he says, "but at least I'm still alive."

It is just before three and the police have the street blocked with the ambulance loading up Ronnie to take him to the hospital, when the tiny traces of snow first begin to stick. At first the flakes linger on windshields and are quickly swept away by intermittent wiper blades, but in a few minutes they begin to faintly collect on the stretches of ground with barren grass and turn the slightest shade of white. It is so slight that if snow had not been forecasted and people didn't have the notion of a chance of accumulation already on their minds they would not notice it being there, but with Sullivan's populace watching and waiting for something to appear, the change in hue does not go unnoticed. It is enough to stir things up again, to cause more doomsayers to rush out into their neighborhoods and into offices and buildings and announce that the end times are near. They call neighbors and acquaintances on their phones and post on Facebook. They turn on their TVs and watch for weather bulletins. Some go out in their yards or to the parking lots outside where they work or shop and study the color of the sky and the shape of the clouds and wait and see if they are possibly the first in town to spot when the first volley of the storm gets underway.

Pete has slept for four hours or so when his phone starts ringing and he knows it's the department wanting him to come back in early. He looks at the clock and sees it is just a few minutes past three and thinks how he should have just come on home this morning instead of going by Betty Hutcherson's place and laying a little pipe. He doesn't know why he went—that's the thing about it. It's not like Betty Hutcherson is any prize anymore, as if she ever was in the first place. She's just available, that's all. Her old man left her ten years ago and she's finally got to the point where she wants a little action, so he pops by whenever their schedules agree. She didn't have to be at work until ten this morning, and he was off by seven, so it was convenient for both of them. But it wasn't like it was anything special. Pete has three or four women in Sullivan he can pay a visit to if he wants. Two of them work at the station, so he has to watch it there. He also has to watch and make sure Martha doesn't find out anything, even if he's beginning to wonder if she would even give a shit if she did.

Thinking of Martha, he wonders if she is going to get off on time today and if she will be home before he has to go back in to work. He looks out the window to see how much snow has fallen and has to strain his eyes to catch any trace of accumulation out there. He sees a small patch on the grill, and maybe there's some snow that's piled up a little on the patrol car, but it's hard to tell since the car is white and twenty-five feet away from the window. There's not so much on the ground that he can see, but the grass is dead and almost white after the winter, so it's hard to tell from looking at it either.

He calls the station and, sure enough, they want him to come back in as soon as he can. It's overtime for him, and though he doesn't really need it for anything it's not like he can say no and turn it down. Whether it snows or not, people are going to be out and clogging up the roads and having wrecks and all that bullshit, so it'll be all hands on deck until the town can get quieted down for the night. He's seen how these sons of bitches act when they think they're fixing to get a blizzard brought down on them, so there ain't nothing to do but get back out there and face the music. He wishes there was some law the department could issue at a time like this and just order everyone to stay their asses at home. It would make everything a whole hell of a lot easier.

Back to Martha, Pete deliberates about what's going on with her right now as he takes his shower and starts getting dressed. Sometimes it's hard to read Martha and other times everything with her is clear as a bell. It's always been that way the twenty years they've been married. One minute he'll be going along with the assumption that everything between them is fine and has been fine for a while and will continue to be fine in the future because that's just the way things are, and then something will appear out of kilter and before he can diagnose what the problem is there are misfires and warning signs popping up all over the place. It's like Martha has two personalities or something. She can go weeks and months being as steady as a clock on a shelf, never losing time, never missing a tick, and then without warning one day he will all at once become aware the ticking is silent and the hands of the clock have stopped moving, and for the life of him he will not know what caused any of this to happen. He will go over what she might have said about her job or what was coming up in her future, and if that analysis gives him no answer, then he will begin to examine his own recent path, wondering if he has not covered his tracks enough during a recent encounter, or if someone may have reported something to Martha about his behavior, or if she is just finally wise to him for good and all the cover-up in the world won't do any good anymore.

The thing about it is nothing has ever been said about what he does or where he goes or anything. As long as he and Martha have been married there has never been any kind of riff at all. He does wonder at times if she is really blind or if he is simply truly remarkable at catting around, and sometimes he even freaks himself out by deciding in his head that she knows what he's been up to and is right around the corner and getting ready to come down on him with a vengeance. But it's not happened yet, and so the feelings will linger for a few days or so and then slowly begin to fade and finally disappear, and he will be free to go about business as usual once again. But there is still always the lingering little doubt in his head that someday the jig is going to be up. He knows how it is when a fellow goes to the well once too often. So he tries to be careful as much as he can muster.

He hasn't seen or heard anything from Martha by the time he gets ready to leave, so he decides to go by the store on his way in to the station. He's tried calling her but no one seems to be answering the phone at Ray's this afternoon. There are some tiny sprinkles of snowflakes on his window, but one brush with the wipers takes care of them. He starts to report in over the radio but decides he'll enjoy a little silence first. God knows he'll have to listen to enough jabbering later on this afternoon and night for him to get his fill of noise.

When he comes over the hill toward the store he sees the three cruisers—which is half the force, including him—parked in the road while an ambulance loads somebody up on a stretcher. It looks to him like somebody stepped out in traffic and got their ass run down. So maybe that's the excuse for all the extra attention. He decides to pull over and join the party and see what's going on. He likes to be up to date on what's going on around the department. If somebody got killed he'd hate to be the last one to know.

Jimmy and Brandon and Eddie are standing by the side of the road, Brandon and Eddie taking a smoke while Jimmy writes a report on his clipboard. Nobody seems too shook up or serious like they might be if somebody had been killed here the last few minutes, so Pete thinks there might not be as big of an emergency going on here as he thought there might be. He leaves his light on and gets out so it will look like he's here on official business too and not just another meddling rubberneck like all these neighborhood folks lining the street watching. For a little bit he'd stop and ask everybody if maybe they might have something better to do than clog up the roadside so people can't get through. He doesn't though, but just walks over and nods at his buddies and waits for somebody to tell him what's going on.

"This guy that got hit was trying to get away after

attempting to pass a bad check," Jimmy says. He looks up to watch the meat wagon load up the suspect. "I've got to go down to the hospital now and finish arresting him if he lives, which I imagine he's going to do."

He walks on over to the ambulance and gets in the back where the kid is. In a minute the siren comes on and the ambulance pulls away. James could keep standing here but there's really nothing left to see.

"How bad was the guy in the wagon?" he asks.

"Hard to say," Brandon said. "He was in and out the whole time I was here. One minute he'd be awake and looking at us, and then he'd close his eyes and be out for a while."

In the back of the ambulance Ronnie is awake and aware but is keeping his eyes closed and acting like he's close to dead, just in case the cop sitting on the bench by his stretcher decides he wants to ask him any more questions or smack him around a little for trying to get away. They still don't know what his name is, since he was careful about bringing anything with his real name or address on it with him when he came to try and cash the check, but he doesn't hold out a whole lot of hope that they're not going to find out all about him before long. The car's back at the vacant lot by the store, so they'll find that and trace it back to his mother, and then the shit will really hit the fan. Technically, the car is hers, since she paid for it. It's not like he's losing a lot if she takes it from him—it's a fucking cheap-ass Escort that isn't worth a shit—but it's all he's got right now. Of course if the shit really hits the fan like he's afraid it's going to, he won't be needing the Escort or any other car for a while. They pretty much don't let you have your car around while you're locked up and doing time.

This is a bunch of shit, he thinks. He makes sure he keeps his eyes closed while he thinks of what to do. He wonders how bad he's hurt. Right this minute it's hard to tell. The best thing to do is stay put with his eyes closed and see what happens when they get to the hospital.

He's beginning to hurt a little at that. He hopes they hurry up and get there.

Pete sees Martha's car is still parked on the hill, even though she was supposed to get off a half hour ago. He starts to park and go inside to see her, but all it takes is one good look at the way the parking lot is filled with cars and he decides to just drive on in to the station. He can call her later if he wants.

Ray has long since deserted the crime scene and gone back inside the store. He figured out right away there was no sense whatsoever standing out on the road talking to the cops and waiting for the ambulance to get there. He just told them he'd press charges if they wanted him to and all they had to do was call him, and then he hustled Larry and himself back inside to get back to work. He couldn't stand being outside imagining all that could be going wrong back inside the store.

He wasn't too far wrong. As the snow started falling a little heavier by the minute the lines at the cash registers in turn began to lengthen, and now it seemed they had almost doubled in their span since he'd first brought up the rear chasing after the forger. Not that his staying inside would have done any good—he doubts five or six more people manning the yoke could have quelled the tide of customers. He looks at the lines and it's almost like he's watching a halftime show, like the customers are all part of a massive marching band and are preparing to spell out in big letters the watchword of the day, which would in this case be, B-U-S-Y. Maybe he should have passed out instruments at the door and appointed someone to be the drum major.

Martha has finished with her instructions to Shirley on checking, and as Shirley took over the register for Lillian she had the feeling she knew enough right this minute to be completely confused. All it took was the first beep of a can as she ran it across the scanner and she knew she was lost. Did she have to listen for the beep each time? She had a little trouble with her hearing anyway, although she didn't like to let it be known much. With all the noise and voices around her and the clattering of the bascarts and the music from that damn elevator station playing through the speakers right above her head she couldn't halfway tell if she'd scanned something or not. What was she supposed to do? Lay her head down on the checklane so she can hear the little beep? Or just assume she'd got it and let it go down the belt with the rest of the order? It could be she was giving things away free, but so what? She didn't ask to be put in this position. She'd been perfectly fine back in the meat department looking at all the people through the one way glass. So it's no skin off her ass.

Trent keeps waiting for his reinforcement crew of part-time checkers and baggers from school to start showing up for work at any time now, but minutes and half hours go by and nobody appears. A couple of times the phone has rung up in the office, but there hasn't been anybody there to answer it. He wonders if somebody is calling in when the phone rings like that and he doesn't know they're not coming in, or if it's just some dumbass on the other end wanting to know how long they are going to be open, what with the snow that's expected to fall and is falling now and is probably going to make the whole town into a winter wonderland. Trent begins having visions of his entire evening crew calling out sick or pulling no shows on him. He can just see himself trying to take care of this whole store by himself while the entire town comes in to strip the shelves. He hasn't seen Fred come in to run the office yet, and neither Lillian's or Paulette's relief have come in either.

This is not looking good at all. He wonders why he answered his phone this morning himself. He should have called Ray and told him there was a good chance he might be having a case of appendicitis. He'd be going to the doctor and letting him know a little later as soon as he found out. But, he'd say to Ray, it doesn't look too good right now. I think the chances are slim to none I make it in for work tonight.

Why didn't he think of that this morning? Now it's too late.

He can't help but keep glancing over at Martha and watching her getting Lillian and Paulette the slightest bit mollified. For a while now he's been expecting either or both of the two to start raising Cain about being stuck in their checklane so long and how somebody needs to do something quick or they might just sign off and go to the back for a while and eat their lunch. Trent, of course, knows neither one of them are the least bit hungry, since both women have a supply of cookies and candy and slim jims and crackers stashed inside their check stand drawers and beside their registers and up in the bag wells that would last them at least a week if they were ever to get truly stranded. The only thing they'd really be bitching about is having to work the whole time they're here. Neither Lillian or Paulette are the least bit used to that. They like to do what they please and that's that. But Martha is handling the situation, just like she always does.

Any minute now he's expecting Lyle to come up front and start bitching about Martha taking his help away, but he doesn't see him yet. Trent knows this lack of controversy and friction is not the result of what a fine Christian man Lyle is, but the lack of histrionics is probably because there is absolutely nothing left to do in the meat department, in which case Lyle is on the most part glad to get rid of his help and be back there alone in the prep room so he can relax and read his fishing magazines while he gets paid for it, or it could be that Lyle is being silent and acting like a team player so he can endear himself to Martha a little more. Trent knows this pose as a stalwart man of the Sullivan Baptist Church only goes so far with Lyle, since Trent would lay odds that if the opportunity to go to bed with Martha ever happened to come his way the deacons meetings and the Wednesday night dinner and prayer services would all be put to rest for the time it took to try and get his rocks off. Trent has crap like this go through his head a little more often these days and it makes him wonder. Is he getting to be Martha's jealous boyfriend here lately? Is he going to let the green-eyed monster eat him up and take over his senses and cause him to do something stupid for the sake of retaining and solidifying his relationship with Martha? It sounds pretty stupid to him, but nonetheless there it is. He can't deny that the thoughts have been running through his brain.

James is back to bagging, wondering while he works if this afternoon would be a good time to ask Mr. Ray for a raise. Because he was the only one in the store who helped Mr. Ray with the check forger it just might be a good time to try. After all, James was the one who grabbed the guy and kept him from running off until the cops came, and the thing of it is the guy would have never got away if the damn cop hadn't told him to let go of his head while James had him in a headlock and fucked up trying to handcuff him to that chair downstairs. Hell, James is pretty sure he'd have caught the little son of a bitch again if that motorcycle hadn't hit him first. If it wasn't for the motorcycle or James the dude would have got away again for sure. One thing for sure is the cop sure wouldn't have caught him, since he was way back there with Mr. Ray. James has seen people in wheelchairs go faster than that.

Bob is thinking about opening the back door and watching it snow for a while until he thinks it's okay to clock out and leave, but right when he has his hand on the lock a woman comes striding into the back room looking back and forth like she needs something. There are signs on the swinging doors from the main floor that say *Employees Only*, but that never seems to stop anybody. They just wander on back into the stockroom as pretty as you please.

She spots Bob over by the door and immediately starts waving her hand for attention, like he can't see all three hundred pounds of her that looks like she ought to be playing defensive end for the Titans up in Nashville.

"Can I help you, ma'am?"

"I'm looking for that produce boy," she says. She's not only wide but she's damn tall for a woman too. Looks like Shaq O'Neil on steroids after a sex change. "Ya'll ain't got a single bag of potatoes out there."

"We're probably out," Bob says, "but I'll look for Lee and ask him."

"I ain't got time to wait around," Ms. Shaq says. "You be a doll and look see what he's got back there, will you?"

"Yes, ma'am," Bob says. He guesses that worthless Lee is up front bagging with everybody else, but as he goes over to the Produce room he looks upstairs and sees Trice and Lee looking down at him. They're smiling because he's got Big Mama right behind him, and this pisses him off to no end.

"Hey," he says to Lee, "where's all your potatoes? You ain't got any on the floor."

"I ain't got none. Ain't going to be any until tomorrow when the truck comes in."

"Tomorrow's not going to do me any good," the woman says. "My family's got to eat today."

"Guess you'll have to go to Kroger's," Lee says. "Kroger has probably got some."

"If I wanted to go to that damn Kroger I'd be there already," the woman says. "I don't like going there. Anyway, that store is all the way on the other side of town, and I ain't got time to do all that traveling."

She gives Lee the most disgusted look she can come up with and walks back out on the main floor.

"Where is Kroger?" Lee asks. "Two fucking miles away? Like that's so fucking far. That goddamn woman can kiss my ass."

"You better not let that woman hear you talking about her like that," Trice laughs. "She'll come back in here and climb these steps and instead of kissing your white ass she'll kick that butt of yours a couple of times."

Lee dons his goofy I don't give a shit grin, like this is what he's been dreaming of all his life.

Ray's been bagging almost ten minutes on the front end, and during that entire time he's only seen Larry and Marcus around helping. Where is Derrick and Trice? Where, as a matter of fact, is Lee? He walks briskly over to the door and looks out in the parking lot for any sign of the three but sees nothing. He tries remembering when he saw them last but can't, so it's definitely been a while. This really gets under his skin, the three of them just disappearing like this when the chips are down and there's a lot to do. He hates to leave the front when it's snowed under like this, so he goes over and starts calling for them on the intercom all to come up front for customer service. He wonders if they are even anywhere where they can hear him. Like a lot of things this day, he feels like he's wasting his time doing something and not even coming close to making any headway and getting anything accomplished.

In a minute or so he sees Trice sneaking up the aisle by the office, looking innocent and attempting to blend back in to all the hustle and activity going on. At the same time to his left here comes Lee up the last aisle, moving along about as slow as a person with two legs can go, smiling like he knows nothing is going to happen to him and he's getting away with whatever he's been doing. Sometimes Ray wishes he could just send Lee home to his mother and let her decide what to do with him for the next ten years, instead of insisting he work at the store and to learn how to be a responsible person. Ray hates admitting it, but he's got news for his wife. This son as a responsible person isn't going to happen any time soon.

He wants to go over and chew Lee out, but there are people waiting at the office window for lottery tickets, so it's going to have to wait until later. He'll have to remember to include Trice in that group too and not just make it a family affair.

"Where's all our afternoon help?" he asks Trent as he passes by. Trent writes the front end schedule every week, so Ray feels like taking his irritation with this entire day out on somebody, and Trent looks like the logical choice. "Don't we have anybody scheduled to come in this afternoon?"

"They're scheduled," Trent says over his shoulder, "but that doesn't mean they're going to show up."

Trice is over at the side of the building peeking around the corner at the black car circling the lot. He is fairly certain whoever is inside the car is looking for him, but it's hard to tell who it is in there because the windows are tinted so much. Trice thinks it might be somebody about some woman he's been messing with, or it could be an unsatisfied customer or even somebody looking to score. It's hard to tell when he doesn't recognize the car from memory. He likes to keep details like that in mind, since they tend to come in handy at times like this. Of course, he could just be getting a little paranoid today and imagining things that aren't really happening. This could just be somebody he doesn't know in a car looking for a parking space. He could walk back inside now and not get in trouble for being missing so long out here in the lot. But it's better to be safe than sorry.

The snow starts coming down a little harder.

Back in her checklane, Lillian looks at the clock and sees she is now thirty minutes past when she was supposed to get off and wonders where her relief is. It's a pretty typical thing for one of those dern kids to be late in the afternoon when it's time for her to get off, so she's accustomed to picking up fifteen or twenty minutes of overtime every day because of it, but once it gets any later than that she starts getting edgy. It's not that she really has anything to do or anywhere to go but home, but she likes getting home early enough to look through the paper and smoke a couple of cigarettes and call a few people from church on the phone to see what's happening in town before she fixes herself something to eat and settles down to watch a few of her programs before she goes to bed for the night. She also doesn't much cotton to the fact that Mr. Ray and Martha just assume she'll keep working until her relief comes in. They could at least come over and ask her.

As a matter of fact she doesn't see anybody coming in to work except for the one little boy who cleans up the meat department at night, and she doesn't even know his name. They've already put him to bagging anyway, so it's not like it's going to help her to go home. She decides she'll give them about fifteen more minutes and then she'll really start raising hell. After all, it's starting to really snow out there. They ought to know she's an old lady, and she needs to get home before it gets too slick.

The sky grows grayer and the sun hides behind the dark foreboding clouds. Snow falls and lingers on the grass and the trees and the sidewalks by the main road in front of the store, and everyone seemed to know that as soon as the sun finished setting the real accumulation was not going to be too far behind. There was nothing anyone could do but get ready.

Ray still had chocolates and flowers and greeting cards on the front display. Nobody was thinking about being anybody's valentine right now.

Trent thought if he could just get out of this register he'd get on the phone and call some of these kids who hadn't showed up yet. He was damned if he was going to go through this night at half-staff.

Martha waited to see if Fred was going to make it in to run the office. He'd called twenty minutes ago and said he was stuck in traffic. Martha thought that was probably a lie.

Lillian fumed and waited.

Paulette kept checking and waiting for one of her men friends to come by and see if she needed a ride home.

Derrick bagged and kept an eye on Mr. Ray. He wanted to go outside and hide out for a while, but it wasn't time to disappear just yet.

Larry wondered if the dude he'd tackled was alive or not. He never meant to get the fucker killed.

Trice made sure he stayed inside and watched the door. He didn't know if that car was still cruising the lot or not.

Lee bags slowly and waits to sneak out the back door. He's got a joint from Derrick in his glove compartment.

Shirley keeps screwing up transactions and having to call Martha over for help. This is really ticking her off, this checking people out shit.

Lyle and Bob talk for a while and then clock out. Lyle's got a deacons' meeting tonight. Bob just wants a beer.

Marcus bags for anybody he thinks might give him a tip.

Pete leaves the station on his way to patrol the south side of town. The south side is where the projects are—two of them—and it can get crazy around there sometimes. But there's maybe snow coming tonight. Maybe it would keep people inside.

Sullivan got ready for the coming of snow.

SIX
5:00 P.M.

Rush hour in the afternoons only lasted a few minutes on a regular weekday in Sullivan, but today was going to be an exception. There was a long line of cars sitting stalled and immobile all the way up the hill in front of the store, and cars waited in line for the privilege of turning into the parking lot and then inching around in a slow-moving circle hoping to find a place to park. Horns honked and flabbergasted disgusted hands drummed impatiently on steering wheels. Occasionally a motorist would grow weary of the waiting and give up the quest, inching their vehicle ever so slowly from the stalled lines until they could press their foot upon an accelerator and peel rubber on the yet-uncovered asphalt and speed away from the unflinching myriad of traffic that showed no promise of ever moving or lightening up in the least.

Derrick leaned against the south side of the building smoking a Newport, wondering where in god's name all these cars were coming from. He didn't think there were that many people in this entire goddamn town.

Trent has had exactly three of his afternoon employees show up so far, and he's afraid that's going to be it for the night. One is a checker and one is a bagger, and the third is this gay kid named Fred who catches the office at night, if by staying on Twitter and Instagram on his phone is an indication of his doing any worthwhile tasks for his pay. But he's at least a warm body. He can answer the phone and issue money orders and lottery tickets. But Trent knows this is not going to be nearly enough to get through the night.

He takes his first checker, Belinda, and puts her in a register behind Shirley, who he lets go home, since he's tired of her screwing up every order she checks out and having to listen to her yell for help from either him or Martha in this bawling vibrating nerve-irritating voice that seems to ricochet off the walls and poke him in the neck and whine in his ears like a hungry mosquito that's somehow got inside your house and won't leave you alone for more than three seconds at a time. Good fucking riddance, he thinks as he watches Shirley head toward the time clock. Go get in your freaking Corolla and get out of my sight. He'd rather stay in this checklane and keep checking all night than listen to her any longer.

So far he's had one checker call and say she had food poisoning and one that said somebody had stolen his car, and no word whatsoever from the two bagboys he hired last week that haven't made it in yet. He knew they both rode the bus, so maybe they were stuck in traffic. They were, after all, from the hood and poor and probably didn't have cell phones to call in and let anybody know where they were, so maybe he could hope they'd be along in a little. But, then again, maybe they'd quit already and would never show at all until Friday to pick up their pay checks. Maybe they were in love and had to romance somebody down in the ghetto because it was St. Valentine's

Day. That was just the way it went around here. You never knew who was coming or going or who you might never see again. Employees just dropped off the radar for no reason.

The car with the tinted windows made its fifth trip around the lot, slowed by traffic almost to a stop. Trice has seen it pretty much each time it made its way around and has made sure he hasn't been seen by whoever is in it in return, since he's all but certain it is him this car is searching for in the first place. In between bagging and trying to stay inside the store as much as possible he's been peeking out the front door and through a small place by the bread rack where a portion of the lot is visible to see if the car is doing anything but circling, and so far that's all that's happened. He sure as shit hopes it stays that way. He doesn't know exactly what he's going to do if he sees it get parked and any of the dudes inside it get out and start to come in the store. He doesn't know who they are or how many there are but he's for certain whoever's inside the car is looking for him. He knows for sure if anybody heads for the front door to come in he's going to be moving toward the back of the store like a frigging cheetah and hope like hell the back door is unlocked and he can get out that way and disappear out through the woods behind the store.

He keeps trying to remember who might be after him right this minute. He's got a few candidates in his mind but he can't say for sure. He keeps trying to narrow down the field.

He's got him a pistol out in his car. He wonders if he ought to take the chance of sneaking out there to get it.

Lee has kept his head down and bagged for close to forty-five minutes since he got called to the front, but it's over an hour now since he was supposed to get off and he's ready to haul his ass out of here. He guesses he could go ask his dad if he could go ahead and leave but he already knows how that would go, so he isn't going to bother with that. He decides what he'll do is sneak back and clock out the first chance he gets, then come back to the front and bag until he has an order he has to take out, and then load the car and leave the bascart in the lot and go get in his car and drive away. The more he thinks about this the more brilliant the plan seems to him. He wonders why it's taken this long for him to come up with such a great idea. He can do it today and get home and change clothes and be gone from the house before his dad ever gets there. He can stay out late and make sure everybody's asleep by the time he comes in. And by tomorrow maybe his dad will have forgotten all about him taking off without asking, and if he hasn't, well, it will be just too damn late for him to do anything about it by then anyway.

"Where is all your meat?" a lady in what looks to be her pajamas asks Ray. "Ya'll ain't got the first thing on the shelf back there."

"We're out," Ray tells her. "Sorry."

"What do you mean out? It's five-thirty in the afternoon. What am I supposed to do about my supper?"

"It's a snow scare," he says. He wonders why he has to explain this. He wonders what rock this woman has been under all day. He'd like to ask her, but that's not the best way for the owner of a business to act. Most times he remembers that, but just for a little while he'd like to forget it today. "We've been bought out."

"Well, when are you going to get some more things in?"

"Not today. Sorry."

He comes out of the office and walks to the back as fast as he can. Maybe, he hopes, this woman and the legion of folks just like her will disappear by the time he gets back.

The milk and eggs and cheese are long gone, just as he'd thought they would be. About the only items holding on in the dairy department is cottage cheese and a scant few containers of yogurt. Canned vegetables and meat are down to stuff like Spam Lite and a scattering of butter beans and yams. He doesn't bother looking at the meat rack or to go see what the produce department might look like by now, since he already knows it's a disaster without wasting his steps to get over there. Maybe there's some frozen food he could possibly get someone to put out and quell the demand some, but when he steps over on aisle six to check he sees the puddle of water in front of the ice cream section and he knows before he sticks his hand inside the glass doors that the freezer has iced up and the compressor has quit working. He goes up and down the coolers anyway feeling for any cold air like a miracle might happen, but all he gets is a warm breeze, like there's some kind of winded dragon trying to take a nap back in the breaker room. He already knows what has to be done, and he wouldn't mind walking away right now and never coming back to it. Everything in the coolers has to be pulled and stored in the back, and he's got to turn everything off and let it all defrost and de-ice for five or six hours, and then when it's working again he's got to work up what hasn't gone to shit back in the shelf and hope the same damn thing doesn't happen again. Of course he's had this problem fixed at least three times in the past year—he's been assured by Clyde and Dave of Truman Refrigeration how he doesn't have to worry about it anymore—but here he is again with who knows how much ruined stock at dinnertime on Valentine's Day when there's a goddamn blizzard on the way, and of course he is royally fucked again. Ray shakes his head. He is not the kind of guy who gets bent out of shape all that often, he is not the sort of man who normally throws a fit and starts ranting and raving and cursing like a sailor, but sometimes enough is enough.

Like this entire goddamn day from hell, sometimes enough is fucking enough.

He walks back to the front end and looks out the door to see if the snow is coming down any harder. He is just in time to see Lee pulling out of the lot in his goddamn Altima. The little worthless son of a bitch, he thinks. The first chance I get I swear to God I'll kill him.

Lillian has just about had it. It is way past time for her to get off and she hasn't seen anybody even make the first step toward trying to relieve her. Hardly any of those sorry part-time kids have come in to work, so it looks like Ray and Martha and Trent are content to let her stay in her checklane until the snow gets through falling or the cows come home or whatever, and it's just about to set Lillian off if it keeps up like this much longer. She would have said something already but she doesn't want to be the first one mouthing off—she'll leave that job to Paulette, who is bound to explode any minute now. Paulette doesn't like to have work interfere with her busy little agenda, so this staying over stuff without being asked isn't going to fly for her much longer either.

Lillian looks up and studies the lines and sees how they're not getting shorter, even though there can't be that much left back in the store to buy. She already knows there isn't any milk or eggs and is sure the meat department is all sold out, so she can't really see what the attraction is for all these people. She feels like telling Ray to make an announcement and lock the doors and go ahead and shut down so everyone can get home safely before all the snow arrives, but she keeps swallowing her impulses down like a pill without water, determined not to be the first one to wave a white flag at all this customer hysteria. Maybe she would if it weren't for the fact that Trent is in a register checking as fast as he can and Martha is still running around trying to help and Ray is darting around like a rabbit on a shooting range trying to keep everything going, so she guesses maybe it wouldn't be the wisest thing she could do adding her name on the shitlist to her bosses later after everything has finally calmed down. But she for damn sure isn't going to try driving home in a blizzard by herself. Somebody was just going to have to take her home tonight.

Derrick has seen Lee pull off and go home and considers doing the same thing himself, but he decides not to, since all it would accomplish would be getting his ass in trouble and maybe getting fired. Maybe Lee can get away with pulling such shit, but he's Ray's son and that has to come into play. Derrick knows his ass would be history if he went and did such a thing, so he tells himself the best thing he can do is keep sacking. This shit has got to end sometime. These fuckers can't keep coming in here forever.

He looks out the window to see if it's snowing any harder. It's getting dark now and it's hard to see.

Paulette has had two of her men friends come in and offer her a ride home, but she's told them she can't leave yet because it's so busy. Check with me a little later on, she'd smiled, knowing they'd both be back within the next hour to see about her again. She knows if push comes to shove she can always get a ride back to her apartment with Trice, but she's not really that up to doing that. Something like that might start giving him ideas about him and her, and he's got enough of them already. She doesn't need to give him any more seeds to start trying to plant.

If Lee had known the traffic was as fucked up as it was he would have never left the store. Hell, instead of sitting in traffic wasting his time he would have done better staying on the clock and making some extra money, but how was he supposed to know that then? All he knew was he was tired of working and wanted to get out of there and maybe go home and take a nap before he went out tonight, because he was tired and the way his dad was riding him all the time he sure as hell wasn't going to get the chance to snooze a little while he was at work.

And he can't take a nap now—not in the middle of sitting in all this traffic. The way he sleeps, when he gets the chance, he might not wake up when the cars in front of him start to move, so he has to stay awake a little longer.

He fiddles around inside his cigarette pack and extracts the skinny joint hidden in there. He hadn't thought he'd have the opportunity to fire it up today, but from past experience he's learned it is always best to be a good boy scout and be prepared. He snickers a little at the thought of this. In his mind he sees himself in a scout uniform with a kerchief around his neck and a backpack hanging from his shoulders, and he's just fished out a number from his pack and is ready to share it with the rest of his troop, who are bored and despondent and don't have a clue how to get through the rest of their weekend camping trip. Lee knows that because he is a good scout himself and has come prepared, and thanks to him, the entire weekend is going to be great. Guys are going to be grinning and earning merit badges and cooking hot dogs on the fire and eating beanie weenies and helping old ladies cross the creek and all that shit. He's pretty much laughing his ass off by the time he fires the joint up.

There's rap music beating out on his radio—he believes it's Drake but he's not really sure—and he turns the volume up so it vibrates the windows, even though he doesn't actually understand the words or know what the song's about. Lee doesn't really like rap that much, but it's what everybody listens to most of the time, so it's okay with him. He doesn't really like music too much at all, if anybody really wanted to know the truth. He especially hated that crap that his dad played over the speakers at work. It was a lot of crap about falling in love and having your heart get broken and shit like that, all getting sung by a bunch of people who sound like they're gasping for air and fixing to die over a bunch of nothing. At least what he's listening to now, even if he doesn't know what the dude is actually saying, he can at least figure the guy is telling the world to kiss his big hairy ass if they don't like what he says or does. Lee likes this. It pretty well sums up exactly how he feels.

Yeah, the world can kiss his ass, all right. That's what he thinks, and he wouldn't mind telling it to a bunch of people too, if they really wanted to know.

This is good shit, he thinks, happy with the quality of weed

Derrick has sold him. The cars move a little and he inches up the road. He's not moving fast enough to please himself, so finally he gets tired of it and jerks the car to the right and tears off on the side of the road where it's just dirt and grass and tries to make it up to the light to turn right, but the road narrows and there's no place for him to go but back into the lane of traffic he just left. He doesn't want to do that, sit in all that mess again, so he turns right onto the hill that's about twelve feet high but not really so steep and attempts to climb up to the parking lot of the Murray Furniture Store that's sitting in the strip mall above. He wishes he had one of those four wheel drive vehicles or something so he could do this a little easier, but the embankment is not that high, so he thinks he can make it.

It's a little exciting to him. The music drums with rap and the windows vibrate and he can feel the Altima's tires churning and plowing up the ground as the car keeps scaling the hill. He's buzzing along with it and having a really good time. This may have been just what he was looking for when he took off from the store. This makes it worth it.

His front tires make it to the asphalt lot with a lurch and a bump, but his rear wheels get stuck some in the dirt and he has to really punch the accelerator to get totally up. The car fishtails and swerves back and forth to the right and the left, and for a minute he thinks maybe he isn't going to make it all the way up the grade after all, but the wheels finally catch and spew up dirt and propel the rest of the car forward. The music plays and he's made it all the way up, and he's really happy and proud of himself until he sees the cop car pulling into the lot with the light flashing on the top, and that's when he knows he's fucked.

Pete sits in his cruiser for a minute after he's got the car blocked in, making whoever the driver is sweat it out a while. He hasn't run the tag yet, but there will be plenty of time to do that later, since he's already decided he's going to run this son of a bitch in no matter what. Somebody's going to have to pay to fix the landscape this asshole has destroyed coming up this hill like that.

Pete gets out and walks over to the car, making a big show out of unbuttoning the strap on his holster so the driver can get a good gander at the pistol he has on his hip. In all his years on the force Pete has never had to fire his handgun, but there's always a first time for everything, so he likes to stay prepared. One of these days he's pretty certain he's going to have to pull it out for something, and that day might just be right now. A fellow can never be too careful.

He motions for the driver to roll the window down. That's when he sees that it's Ray Jenkins' boy. Pete knows the kid from coming in the store to see Martha to get his morning honey bun. He's never really had any dealings with him, but he maybe has to reevaluate exactly how he's going to handle this. He doesn't want to do something right off the cuff that might piss Martha or her boss off.

Lee looks out the window at him with a stupid silly grin on his face, and Pete doesn't need to go get his PhD in Human Behavior to know this kid is on something. Pot immediately comes to Pete's mind, since the odor escaping from the car window is enough to knock him over. He doesn't know if it's going to be possible to sweep this under the rug and let this kid off easily or with just a warning, not with the way the hill has been torn up and this kid is sitting in the car out of his tree and obviously impaired too much to drive home safely. Most of the time Pete would relish an opportunity to run somebody in during an occurrence like this, but now he's caught between a rock and a hard place. He's going to have to think this one over a few times before he acts.

"I need to see your license and registration," Pete says. "Also proof of insurance. Then I need you to get out of the car."

Lee makes a big production out of looking for his registration in the glove compartment, then turning around and acting apologetic when he can't seem to find it. He knows it's probably in there someplace but he doesn't want to go through a big production like emptying everything out of there to look for it, because then the possibility would be this cop is going to see the rolling papers he's got stuffed in there among the napkins and papers and everything else. It's best, Lee decides, to just act like he doesn't know where it is right this minute.

Anyway, he knows who this cop is. He's Martha's old man; Lee sees him in the store a lot. He wonders if it would be to his advantage to bring this fact up, or if the guy might go off on him if he thought Lee was trying to butter him up. Lee's confused as hell right now. He doesn't know whether to open his mouth or not.

"I was trying to get home quick before it snowed," he finally says.

"Yeah," Pete says. "I noticed how much of a hurry you were in. I guess you figured it was fixing to be a blizzard." Pete shakes his head. "Get out of the car and stand over there," he says, pointing toward the rear fender.

Pete watches the kid fold himself out of the car. He

wonders whether he should handcuff him or not. He could put him in the cruiser while he searches the car. He decides to talk to him a minute first. Then he'll decide which way he needs to go with this.

"I know you from Ray's," Pete says. "As a matter of fact I saw you this morning when I was in there, so I guess you just got off a few minutes ago and you're on your way home. Am I right?"

"Yes sir," Lee says, doing his best to be polite for maybe the first time in five years. "I got off about twenty minutes ago. I had to pee and I was just sitting there in traffic and couldn't stand it anymore. That's why I did what I did."

"I don't know if I believe you or not," Pete says. "I don't know if I trust you telling me the truth, because I'll just let you know something. I ain't ever had to piss that much in all my life, and I'm a hell of a lot older than you."

Lee just stands there and looks stupid. He's smart enough to know that the best thing he can do is not open his mouth.

Trice is not about to go outside now. He's watched this car keep circling around the lot, idle in traffic, park once or twice and sit, and now he's absolutely certain this isn't any vehicle full of shoppers worrying about a big snowfall that's coming, and it ain't any dude with a thorn bush up his ass wondering what he's going to get his woman for Valentine's. This for sure is somebody searching for somebody to do something to, and of all the candidates on the property of this store right this minute, Trice deducts he is probably the most likely brother for somebody to be looking for. Like it's been running through his mind for the last hour or so, he doesn't know exactly what it is somebody's after for him for, but he's pretty sure he's the one who needs to be worried. He keeps looking out the door and spotting the car, then measuring how far away his own car is from where the other is parked, and if it's a good bet he can make it to his car and get out of the lot before he gets spotted by whoever it is out there who might just be wanting to kill him.

The thing he's really trying to figure out is does whoever this person out there wanting to mess him up know what kind of car he's driving? Are they going to know it's him when his car goes tearing out of here in a minute?

"Don't you run out of here real fast when you get ready to leave," Paulette says to him. "I just may be needing a ride home, the way it looks. I ain't about to try and take that bus home in no snow."

This is about all Trice needs right now, and it plays with his mind. He's been waiting for the chance to get Paulette off by herself away from this store, and this snow scare going on this evening is presenting him an excellent opportunity, but he doesn't know how any of that is going to play out with this damn car out in the lot that may or may not want his ass dead.

He doesn't want to tell Paulette anything about the car, so he just shakes his head and agrees with her for the time being, hoping he'll think of a good plan in the next few minutes.

Ray walks outside after the automatic timer lights have come on to see what the weather is doing. He can see a fine little mist coming down up by the floodlights, but he can't really tell if it's sleet or snow or just the slightest trickle of rain. He doesn't see anything collecting on the ground or on the windshields of the cars in the lot, and he looks out on the street and sees the cars are still fairly lined up. He notices how his lot is still full but there aren't any cars circling looking for a place to park like they had been for the last couple of hours, and then he walks back inside and he can see the back of the checkout lines, which is something he hasn't seen since early this morning.

He moves over to the display table and starts marking down the candy and the flowers. If he doesn't get rid of this stuff tonight he's going to be stuck with it all week.

Ronnie the forger wakes up in a bed with his arm in a cast. His head hurts like hell and his nose feels like it's completely stopped up. He looks around and sees he's in some kind of hospital room without windows where he can't get up and look outside. He doesn't think he can get up anyway, so it's all right. He closes his eyes and goes back to sleep.

Pete has Lee in the back of his car. The kid is high as a kite, and Pete is debating whether to run him in or take him back to the store and let his dad deal with him. He knows he'll get brownie points from Martha if he takes him to Ray, but he's not really worried about it that much. He's trying to decide what will save him some paperwork and court time. He hasn't got time for a lot of bullshit. He knows if he searches the car he's probably going to find something, then it will be Katy bar the door for this night. He decides not to look.

Lillian has been at work eleven hours now. Paulette is right behind her at ten. Martha was here before both of them, so she knows all the two of them are waiting on before they start raising the roof is for her to leave. She's tired too, but she's going to try and hang on for a few more minutes, making sure the office is all right before she leaves. The business looks like it's starting to die down. Outside it looks like maybe the snow has missed them after all. It's hard to tell because it's so dark. Maybe another half hour and they'll know for sure.

A part-time checker actually shows up for work, and Trent takes the opportunity to put her in the checklane behind him. Now he has two checkers, so he goes and blocks off Lillian's and Paulette's lanes so they can go home. It looks to him like the business is dying off. He's got two baggers and someone to watch the office. There's no stock to work whatsoever, nothing to do back in meat or produce. The only way the store will have milk and eggs tonight is for him to drive out to somebody's farm and bring back a cow and a hen. What he really needs to happen is to empty this store of customers—since there's nothing for them to buy anyway—and get all the early help out of here and on their way home. This includes Ray. As soon as he can get that accomplished he can get the floor swept and spot-mopped, and maybe close up early and let everybody go home. He knows Ray won't care. He'll be saving money on hourly wages if that happens, especially since there won't be any customers coming in for anything.

Not because they'll be snowed in or anything like that, because nothing is happening outside that he can see. It looks like the storm may have passed them by.

SEVEN
7:30 P.M.

It wasn't two minutes after Trent finished telling the day crew they could all go home when the snow started coming down again like somebody had flipped a switch. He started to tell them all to hold on a minute, to maybe have them clock back in and keep them there, but it was only an hour and a half anyway until closing time, so he thought he could make it without doing that. The store was empty of both customers and product now, so what could possibly go wrong in ninety minutes? Anyway, he didn't want to see the look on Ray's face when he realized Trent had panicked and had a bunch of people standing around on the clock doing nothing. No, screw that. Trent would rather suffer a little while rather than deal with skinflint Ray on such a subject as that.

Martha was more than glad to leave. She'd been at work a little more than thirteen hours and she hadn't taken so much as a break all day, so she couldn't tell if she was hungry and famished more than she was exhausted. Thirteen straight hours is a long time for anybody to have to work, even if they're sitting at a desk the entire time, which she hadn't been doing, and even if they were young and full of boundless energy and enthusiasm, which, while she still had energy and enthusiasm way above average for a person her age, still she was forty-five and her days of hopping around incessantly like a spring chicken were over and done. She needed to get home and get her feet up. She needed something to eat. She remembered how her day had not just started with work this morning either. There was also the fact that she had stayed at Trent's apartment last night, and sleep had been limited then. It was no wonder she was tired.

Ray has just finished marking down all the Valentine merchandise on the display table and making a mental estimation in his head on how much money he is going to lose on this holiday because of the snow scare and the panic and the major fact that the people here in this poor side of Sullivan were probably the most un-romantic human beings that ever walked the face of the earth. Hell, he could drive down the interstate an hour and go to the Memphis Zoo and find giraffes and elephants and chimpanzees that had more romance and sentimentality in their souls than these folks. He told himself to remember all this next year when the holiday rolled around again and not go overboard buying a bunch of crap that was just going to go to waste.

It was about then when he remembers he hasn't done anything for Valentine's Day for his own wife. He had told her last night to think of some restaurant she might like to go out to for dinner, and he would call her during the afternoon to make plans. Well, it was coming up on eight now, and he hadn't made that call yet. He wondered if he should pick out some of the marked-down candy and flowers and take them home with him. He could tell her how the day had gone to shit and he'd never been able to stop. Probably she would understand. Her daddy had been a grocery man, and she'd been married to Ray thirty-three years. She had a good inkling about holidays and snow scares and such.

He is deliberating on this very thing when he sees Lillian coming from the back time clock with her coat on and hears her tell him good night. He starts to respond, but then he notices how she's stopped at the door and is looking out, like she is frozen to the spot by some monster that has taken residence in the lot. Ray wonders if perhaps there is some altercation going on out there or if somebody has a gun or whatever, so he leaves the Valentine's display table and walks over to see what is going on.

"Oh my god," Lillian says. "I wish you would look at that."

The snow is coming down again in fat pregnant flakes and it's hard to see too far from where they are standing. The street and the traffic have vanished from view and it's difficult to even see how many cars are still in the lot. It hasn't been snowing long, but this doesn't look good to Ray.

"There's not any way at all I can drive home in this," Lillian says. "There's a hill in front of my house, and I'll never be able to get down it without ending up in a ditch. I should have already been home before this mess got started."

She looks over at Ray like this is all his fault, that he is guilty of endangering her life, and he knows he has to say something to get himself off the hook she's trying to hang him from.

"You just leave your car here tonight," he tells her. "I'll take you home in just a few minutes." He knows she's fixing to add something to this offer, so he goes ahead and says the rest so he doesn't have to listen to it. "I'll pick you up in the morning too. You don't have to worry about that either."

"I wouldn't bet on you being able to get down that hill," Lillian mumbles. She wants to make sure Ray and everybody else pays the price of making her stay late tonight, for keeping her from getting home safe and sound. "You don't know how bad that street can get."

Paulette gets to the door and sees the snow too. Trice brings up the rear behind her, but he doesn't much look like he's ready to leave just yet. It is almost as if he is glad to see this blizzard enveloping them so suddenly. It is like God has provided him with a good excuse to not go outside right this minute. He thinks maybe if the snow comes down like this for a while then maybe the car out in the lot with the person or persons in it who may or may not want him dead might get frightened of not being able to get away and will leave before the awful deed gets finalized, whatever horrible terrible scary thing it is that he or she or they have had in mind. Trice is just fine with hanging out a while longer.

"We better go ahead and go before it gets worse," Paulette says. "You act like it's going to get better if we keep standing here."

"It's coming down pretty heavy," Trice says, peering out the glass. "My wipers ain't all that good. I'm afraid I might not be able to see."

The two part-time checkers lean on their checkstands and fold their arms, since there are no customers in the store for them to check out. One checks her phone for texts. One bagger is eyeing the marked-down candy, while the other has disappeared somewhere. Up in the office Fred is talking on the phone, and who knows if the call is business-related or not? Ray wonders where Trent is, why he's not up here giving these kids something to do. This is not going to do the store budget a bit of good having all this help in here and not a one of them lifting a finger. He starts to say something, but he's got a few other things on his mind at the moment. There's a lot going on he needs to see to before he can leave.

The two of them may have been at the store together all day, but there hadn't been the first free minute for them to talk, so when Trent sees Martha getting ready to leave he stops her before she goes back on the main floor and lightly touches her on the elbow. She stops and looks up at him with a smile.

"Some day, huh?" she says.

"Yeah, I'll say it was. I don't know when I've ever had this much fun before."

"At least you got a lot of checking practice in. Now, the next time someone calls out sick I'll know who to call."

He looks around to see if there's anyone around, and when he sees they're alone he takes his hand and rubs her arm a little. He's tired from this day, but he's not all that tired. He's still got energy for something else.

"I saw your old man in here when I came in. I guess he was hungry or something. I decided the best thing to do was go to the back until he left."

"He was just getting something to eat before he went home. He'd just got off."

"I was afraid he was wondering where you'd been last night. I thought he might have tried to call you or something."

"No. He was just stopping by on his way home. He didn't say anything."

"Are you going to try and go home now?"

"I think I'd better," Martha said. "I'm pretty tired, and I'm not so sure what hours he's going to be working tonight. They called him back in early, so he might get off earlier if the snow doesn't get too bad."

"It's starting to really come down now," Trent said, "so you'd better hurry up and be on your way."

"I didn't know it was snowing again. I thought it had stopped."

"It just started again."

Pete pulls into the lot with Lee in the back seat. It's not all that often that Pete decides to cut a guy a break, and he for damn sure knows this kid in his back seat hasn't really done anything to deserve one, but there is something in him that says he can keep things really simple by dumping this problem back in Ray Jenkins' lap and being done with it on his part. Not only will he not have to fill out a report or go to court on his off day, but it will make him look good to Martha and a lot of people and keep anybody from saying bad things about him or pointing out some assorted shitty things he's done every now and then in the past that hasn't really made him a lot of friends. Pete knows he doesn't truly need any more friends to his credit, but it never hurts to have people think you're not such a bad guy in the long run after all.

He goes around and opens the door to let Lee out and watches him climb out. He hasn't put cuffs on the kid even though it's against policy not to do so, but since he knows the kid isn't packing or getting ready to do harm to anybody he's decided to let it slide and just carry him back down here. He figures he can chew his ass out in front of his old man and get it all over with. He wants to go ahead and get this done quickly, because the snow is starting to really come down now and he knows his radio is fixing to light up with activity. People in this town will be killing themselves for sure if it keeps on snowing like this.

Derrick leaves everybody standing at the door and gets ready to walk home. Everybody else may want to stand around and watch the snow come down, but not him. He knows the longer he waits around the better chance there is Mr. Ray decides to have everybody clock back in and do a little more work. Derrick can imagine more fools getting in their cars and trying to come in and shop some more, what with all this snow falling like crazy, and he doesn't plan to still be standing here being a part of it when it happens. He doesn't need anybody to give him a ride home either—his momma's house isn't that far away, just across the lot and through the vacant woods behind the store, then a couple of houses up the street. He can be home inside of ten minutes.

He tells everyone good night and takes off down the sidewalk in the snow. The walk isn't too slippery yet, but he keeps his head down and pays attention in case he hits a slick patch and falls on his ass with everybody watching. He doesn't have a hat or a parka, so he pulls his jacket up to cover his head so the snow doesn't pile up in his hair and give him a good case of pneumonia. The wind isn't blowing much and it's not really that cold, but that doesn't mean he likes being out in this. He could give a good rat's ass if he ever saw snow again in his life. He just wants to get home and see if there's anything to eat, if his mother has cooked anything for him tonight or just ate one of them TV dinners she likes so much. She don't cook for him or his brothers like she used to. Derrick guesses she may be getting too old to fool with it that much.

Somebody's thrown some old tires out back right before the asphalt of the lot ends, and he almost stumbles over a hubcap that's covered in snow in the grass. He has to really be careful through this stretch when he first enters, because people pitch shit out and dump crap back here all the time. Most of the times it's just plain old trash and rubbish, but a couple of times he's had to stop and look at what he came across. There was a bicycle somebody had run over with a car. He'd seen a guitar laying in the grass and thought he'd really come across something good, but there was a hole in the back as big as a basketball, so he'd just let it stay there. One time there was a paint can and he wondered if it had even been opened, then when he picked it up it was full of dead kittens. He just tried to step around the mess now. He was sure there was never going to be any kind of treasure left behind back here worth trying to salvage.

He decides he might have him a little reefer out here under this tree before he goes home. The snow can't get to him under the branches and he can relax a minute without having to talk to his mother or his brothers and listen to all their bullshit. Besides, getting a little toked will make his supper taste a whole lot better, even if it is a TV dinner.

He fires up his number and rests his back against the tree. He's had to work about twice as hard and twice as long today as he's accustomed to, and damn if he isn't tired for a change. Usually a day at the store is like a walk in the park or something. He can catch up on his conversation with people, sell a little reefer here and there, and maybe even bone up on a few tips too. This snow scare Valentine's Day work your assend off shit ain't going to fly too much for him on a regular basis. Next time he sees something like today in the works he'll just save a lot of heartache and trouble and call out sick the very first thing.

From where he is standing he can see the back of the store and the back dock where the big trucks back in to get unloaded and the vendors bring in their orders. There's two dumpsters in between the ramp and the dock that stay full most of the time, both from the store and whoever in the neighborhood wants to be ecologically correct and throw all their junk in the dumpster and not back in the lot where Derrick is taking deep hits on his joint. He is studying something in the left dumpster that appears to be a car bumper because it is somewhat silver like chrome and it glistens a little beneath the floodlights that shine on the back of the store to try and keep people from breaking in overnight when no one is around. There's an alarm that goes off back there too if somebody comes up and jiggles the door to see if it might budge; it goes off and you can hear it a mile off, all over the neighborhood. Derrick has heard it before from his own bed, and he's way on up the street behind the lot. It's enough to scare the piss out of anybody trying to get in and not expecting it to be there all of a sudden shrieking out into the air like it does.

He sees this same car pull around from the other side of the building and sit there a minute with the motor running and exhaust coming out of the two taillights like it's a horror movie back there and some monsters are fixing to materialize and come out from all that fog looking to find somebody to kill. This is the fourth or fifth time Derrick has seen this car in the past hour or so, so it doesn't take much for him to think whoever is inside there is up to something. The first thing that comes to his mind is Trice, but of course that doesn't mean he's a genius or he's psychic or anything. Trice is always into something—Derrick isn't the only one in the world who knows that. You see something like this car or maybe some dude got a scowl on his face looking around the store and the first thing you think of if you've got any sense is Trice and what kind of shit he's got himself into this time. The boy is a walking poster child for trouble, and it seems like it's something new all the time. This is one reason Derrick doesn't have too much to do with him outside of work. You hang with that mother, Derrick thinks, and you got a good chance of getting involved in some bad shit just by being in the vicinity.

"Are we going or not?" Paulette asks. "We keep standing here watching it snow and we ain't going to be able to get anywhere. We might as well just get cozy and spend the night."

"I'm hoping it will slack off in a minute or so," says Trice. He steps up as close as he dares to the door and looks out to see if he sees that car again. Right now he doesn't, but he wants to make sure.

Larry doesn't wait around for Mr. Ray to change his mind because the snow's coming down so hard. He shoulders his way past everyone grouped at the door and mumbles good night as he leaves. Any minute he's expecting somebody to call him back, but he doesn't hear anything and keeps on walking. He's looking for that same car Trice is scanning the lot for, and he knows why Trice doesn't want to come outside just yet. Somebody's after Trice's ass, Larry knows, and he just hopes they're not watching him right now walking through the lot for the road and thinking he might be Trice. He for damn sure doesn't want to get his ass in a sling because somebody thinks he's Trice. Hell no, Larry thinks. He's got enough trouble without adding that kind of shit on to it.

He keeps on walking expecting trouble, but nothing happens. He feels better with every step he takes. When he gets to the street he is tempted to start running just to make sure he's safe, but he doesn't want to attract attention. With his luck some cop will come along and think he's running from something and haul him in.

Larry spends so much time being careful that it makes him tireder than hell sometimes.

He still can't help but look back over his shoulder at the store and the lot just to see if anything is happening. From where he stands on the street, he can see the car he's been watching parked back by the dock at the back of the building.

The last thing in the world Larry wants to do right now is go back to the store, but he knows as good as he's standing out here in the falling snow that if he doesn't something bad is going to go down. He's seen it happen too many times before. It could be it's not going to help anything for him to go back, but maybe it will keep Trice inside and whoever is in the car will get tired and leave. But he doubts it. They can see Trice's car parked out there in the lot, so they know he hasn't left yet. It looks to Larry like they're going to be patient and stick around.

He turns around and starts walking back down the hill. There aren't but about two cars in the lot he doesn't recognize, so he knows the store isn't busy at all. He sees Martha's car and Lillian's and Mr. Trent's and Mr. Ray's besides Trice's Impala out front. Maybe one of those other cars belong to some of the part-timers; he's not sure. He's usually never around when most of them come in, so he doesn't know if they've got cars or not. Probably not. Most of them don't have the dough. Most of them live over in the hood.

The other car, the Chrysler, is still sitting out there. It hasn't moved. Larry decides he'd better hurry up and get back to the store.

"It doesn't look like we're going to get that much more business tonight." Trent has come from the backroom and is standing beside Ray at the door, trying to put a thought into Ray's head. "If we get the store emptied out in the next few minutes and get swept and mopped we can close up early and get out of here before it gets too bad. There sure isn't any stock we can work."

"You could have everybody face the aisles. We look like a tornado hit us."

"More like a hurricane and an earthquake combined," Trent says, "but if you ask me, there's not a whole lot we can do to make it any better tonight."

"You may be right," Ray says. He looks around the store and the only thing that looks like it's well-stocked is the Valentine display. "It may be best to just get out of here in the next few minutes and get these kids on their way home. Ain't any use in anybody getting stranded."

"I'll take them home if they don't have rides," Trent says, though he sure hopes it doesn't come to that. He's really not that into risking his life and his car for two or three part-time kids. Ray doesn't pay him enough for that kind of stuff.

He sees a police cruiser has pulled into the parking lot

without its flashing lights on, so Trent thinks it's Martha's old man coming by to check on her. He sees it is Pete when Pete gets out of the car, but then he watches him walk around to the back of the cruiser and open the far door to let somebody out. When Lee stands up Trent watches Pete take him by the arm like Lee is a recalcitrant first grader and lead him up to the front door. Lee doesn't look very happy about this.

To go with the rest of this day, Lee getting out of the back seat of a patrol car is about the last thing Ray wants to see right now.

"Lee," Paulette says, "what've you done now?"

"I thought I'd bring your boy by to you," Pete says to Ray. "He got himself into a little pickle on his way home."

Trice, standing inside the door, has never been so happy to see a cop in his life.

At the back of the store Derrick is good and ripped leaning back against his tree. He's already seen the cop car pull in the lot, and he's watching the parked car in front of him back up without its lights on and pull around to the opposite side of the building so it won't be seen. Derrick knows they're fixing to head down the alley and take off. They won't be back tonight. One thing for sure, though, is he's not going back to the store to find out what's going on. Fuck that shit. The last thing he wants to see tonight is a damn cop. He didn't stand out here in the goddamn snow for any of that noise. It might be Martha's old man that's down there, but it's still a cop. No, he decides. My ass is on the way to the house.

Trent decides since Pete is now on the scene it is a good idea for him to walk the store and see what needs to be done before closing up. He notices how Martha has just stood there with concern on her face about what's going on with that worthless Lee and never looked his way one time once Pete got in the door, which is more than fine and dandy with Trent. It wasn't like he was going to have anything to do with Martha tonight anyway, so he thinks the farther he vacates the front end where all the action is the better it will go for everybody. He'll just go do something else and let everybody else work out the kinks.

The farther he gets from the front and the closer he gets to the backroom the better he feels. Now, if everybody would just leave he'd be in terrific shape.

Pete lays it out for Ray the best he can. He wants to get this over and done with, taken care of satisfactorily, and walk away knowing Ray owes him one for not running his kid down to the station. He doesn't say anything about his suspicions that there are probably drugs in the car someplace, but he lets him know about everything else.

"I'm going to write him a ticket for making an illegal turn and destruction of property, so if you take care of the damages before the court date I'll make sure everything gets dropped from the docket. That's about all I can do for you."

"Thank you, Pete," Ray says. "I'll take care of it tomorrow first thing."

"You better keep your nose clean from here on out," Pete says to Lee. "If I didn't know your daddy I'd run you in for sure."

Pete walks up to where Martha is standing. She is half-looking out at the snow and half-eavesdropping on what has been going on with Ray and Lee and Pete, so he is glad she has been able to witness the favor he's just bestowed upon her boss. This is the kind of thing that will earn him some more leeway down the road sometime, because it's not like she can say he is an out and out bastard one hundred percent of the time, since she and her co-workers have now witnessed him doing something nice like this.

"That snow's getting bad out there," he tells her. "Do you want me to drive you home or just follow behind you to make sure you get there all right?"

"I think I can make it," she says.

"I'll be right behind you."

At the same time Martha and Pete leave Trice decides it is a good idea for him to go too, and he walks out quickly toward his car, sticking as close to Pete as he can. He has gone out the door so fast he has forgotten all about Paulette, who rushes to catch up with him.

"I told you I needed a ride," she says. "First you stand there like you're afraid to drive, and then you act like you can't wait to get to your car. You act about half crazy sometimes."

Larry watches everyone pull off. He doesn't see the other car anywhere around, so he guesses it's safe right now. He takes off walking up the road again.

EIGHT
8:30 P.M.

Trent didn't think Ray was ever going to leave. He kept watching Ray go to the back and come back up to the front with his jacket on, and then he'd mumble something under his breath and disappear toward the back again. The first time Trent saw him over in the last aisle messing with the frozen food cooler, and Trent could only hope against hope Ray wasn't planning to try and take care of trying to fix the cooler tonight. He had already managed to get the compressor to kick back on—wasn't that enough? Yes, some of the ice cream had been beyond saving but it was still a minor miracle there was still even some that was salvaged sitting in the freezer, so why should Ray tamper with it now? There was always tomorrow, and anyway, the hordes had bought most of the ice cream in the condition it was in, half unthawed. They had scooped it into their carts and took it home pretty as you please, so all's well that ends well is what Trent thinks. It looked to him like they had come out smelling like a rose in the whole deal. He starts to go back and tell Ray exactly that, but when he goes that way Ray is gone and over in the first aisle checking on the dairy. Trent wants to alert Ray to the news flash he's obviously missed. There are no eggs. There is no milk. There is nothing back there to check.

Why don't I just go home first, Trent thinks, and let Ray close up? He's obviously going to be here anyway.

But Ray is back up front with his jacket on again. He holds up one finger to Lillian to tell her one minute more and then stops to take another fleeting look at the Valentine's Day display, which more or less looks just the same as it did this morning.

"We're hung on a lot of this stuff," he tells Trent sadly. "I had a bad feeling when I ordered them flowers. I knew they wouldn't sell. I don't know what I was thinking of." He looks over at the door where Lillian and Lee are standing. "I never have tried selling roses before, but I thought maybe we could make a little extra profit on them this time." He shakes his head. "I knew better. I don't know what I was trying to prove."

"The snow scare ruined the holiday," Trent offers. "People got so wound up about the storm they didn't even think about Valentine's Day. They were too worried about eating and getting home safe."

"Yeah," Ray says. "Speaking of that, I've got to get Lillian home before she has a nervous breakdown. Then I've got to deal with Lee. I guess you heard what he's been up to tonight."

"I heard."

"I ought to kill him. Maybe I will. It could solve a lot of problems, you think?" A small grin flicks across Ray's face. "Soon as you get everybody out of here close up and go home. There's nothing else we can do tonight."

No hock, Sherlock, Trent thinks, but he shakes his head in agreement and watches Ray and Lee and Lillian go out the door. Now he's left with five part-timers all standing around waiting for him to tell them to clock out. Why should he be the one to disappoint them? There's maybe a few more orders back in the aisles, so as quick as he can herd them out he'll lock up. He goes over and locks the In door and shuts off the outside lights. The snow is still falling, just not as hard. If he can get out of here in a few minutes he can be home before the evening news starts. That sounds like a plan to him.

When they get to Ray's Blazer Ray tells Lee to get in the back seat and let Lillian ride up front. Ray knows that Lillian is none too happy leaving her Camry at the store overnight, so he tries to fill up the silence in the car by turning on the radio, something he never does. Most of the time he prefers riding into work in the mornings and going home in the evenings in abject silence, which gives him a chance to reflect on how he might do something or have done something to improve the store somewhat this day, something for which in the total quiet inside the cab he never seems to find an answer. The music that comes out of his speakers right now is some form of country he has never heard. He does not know the song. He does not know the singer. He wonders if what he is hearing is even country, even if the announcer has proudly proclaimed it to be so and even played a jingle with a singing duo asserting it is of the genre. He doesn't know which is worse, the silence or the noise, and he wishes Lillian would say something so he doesn't have to decide what it is tonight.

"Do you mind if I smoke, Ray?" Lillian asks. "Riding along on all this ice makes me nervous as a cat."

"Go right ahead."

He looks in his mirror and sees Lee has already lit a

cigarette and is blowing smoke rings at his window. He never asked at all, Ray thinks. Even when he's in deep trouble he just goes ahead and does what he pleases. Maybe he should have just told Pete to run him in. Maybe it would have taught him a lesson. But he doubted it.

Going up the hill isn't too bad. The tires don't slide and Ray never goes into a fishtail or anything. It also helps that there isn't much traffic out. He supposes everyone is home safe and sound and riding out the storm by now, which is what he hopes he is doing very soon. But he's got to get Lillian home first.

Going down the hill is where it begins to get a little bit dicey.

Ray has to make certain not to start going too fast and he has to remember to tap on his brakes a little as he goes down, which is easy to do until he comes up on somebody in a small egg-shaped car of indeterminate make whose driver has decided the best way to slow down to make a left into a Mapco at the intersection is to jam on the brakes with all their might and see if this might help the car to keep from sliding on by the red light and going into the intersection without stopping, which it doesn't. Luckily, there are no other cars around, so the little piece of overpriced dung finally slows to a stop and sits sideways against a curb, looking for all the world like it is confused by what it had just gone through and wouldn't mind in the least if its driver would park it and call a taxi or take a bus home and leave it there for the night.

"I guess you see what I mean now," Lillian says. She sounds like she's pleased with the trouble Ray is having on the roads. It occurs to Ray that about the only way she could get more ecstatic would be for him to have a wreck. For a moment he wants to forget that he is her employer and a mature adult. What he would like to do is send his car into a spin and swerve at about sixty miles an hour and see how much old Lillian enjoys it when they are hurtling along sideways in a slide heading toward a big ditch that's ready to gobble them up, then he could see how pleased she is at the predicament he's in.

But he doesn't. He tries to understand how it is with Lillian, with her being a widow and having a daughter in prison for mixing meth and a son who's about half drug addict himself who spends about a day a week hoisting things out of Lillian's house and pawning them off so he can make another payment on his truck. It's not any wonder Lillian comes to work with a chip on her shoulder sometimes, and it's not any big surprise that she would like--after thirty-something years around this store, being here before everyone else was, being here before Ray bought the place from the Millers sixteen years ago--that everyone might show a little deference toward her on a regular basis, that folks might have some respect for the time she's put in and the knowledge she's imparted and all the hard work she's done to make the store successful. Ray knows a good bit of this is bullshit because Lillian sure as hell doesn't kill herself working and doesn't ever offer anything useful unless it's beneficial to her, but he still has to admit she's dependable and mostly honest and she's got a goodly portion of customers who like her and go to her for things, so Ray wants to keep her around and do his best to try and make her happy.

Or at least not muttering all kinds of shit under her breath and using her wiles to make everybody else who works in the store look bad.

So he's careful getting her down her hill and home. He even has Lee go with her up the sidewalk and up the steps and make sure she gets in the door okay.

"I'll call you in the morning," he says from his window. "If you want me to I can come and pick you up."

He already knows what the answer to that is going to be, but he says it anyway. It's like the part he has to play to keep her happy. He knows in the morning when he calls Lillian will tell him how slick the hill is and how he'll never be able to make it down or back up until it melts, so Ray will say fine, and Lillian will take the day off and Ray will have to get Paulette to come in early and find a second checker to work during the day. This is par for the course, so he doesn't worry about it too much tonight. This is just something Lillian does from time to time that he and everyone have learned to expect and accept. Every now and then Lillian is going to not come to work just to show Ray and everybody else how valuable she is and how everybody in the whole town of Sullivan misses her when she isn't there. Then she does something like come in on a Saturday when she's usually off to make up the time she's missed.

So be it, Ray thinks. He doesn't understand it and he never will, but that's the way it is and he doesn't think it will change until somebody drops dead or the world ends.

Paulette keeps looking over at Trice and wondering what he's doing. She hasn't said anything yet, but already Trice has taken about three turns that are definitely the wrong direction on the way to Paulette's apartment. She wonders if he's getting ready to try and pull some trick on her, like take her to his place and try to make a move on her or something, but she doesn't really think that's what is happening. She just thinks he's acting funny. She knows Trice well enough to know when he's acting up and when he's in trouble over something. He does one or the other all the time, so it's easy to tell the difference.

He keeps looking in his mirror, like he's a lot more worried about what's behind him than he is the snow and the ice on the street and the parked cars here and there that have been abandoned and left behind by their drivers, some of them sideways and sticking out into the street just waiting for somebody to come along and plow into them. Paulette hasn't driven a car in about three years now, not since she had the wreck that totaled her car and neither she nor the other driver had insurance, but she can tell the snow isn't too bad on the streets just yet. She'd like Trice to stop fooling around and hurry up and get her home, but she'd like to know what's going through his head first. She knows something's going on for sure.

"What are you looking for in that mirror?" she finally asks. "I know you think you're real pretty, but you ain't that handsome where you have to look at yourself all the time. Plus, I don't need no tour of the town either. I've lived here thirty years and I know what's here. All I want to do is get myself home."

"To tell you the truth, I'm looking to see if anybody's following me. I've had some people watching me down at the store tonight."

"My god, boy. What have you gone and done this time?"

"I ain't sure what they want. I've been trying to figure it out."

"Well, I sure wish you'd have told me before I got in this car with you. I don't want to be in the middle of a whole lot of trouble just because I'm riding with you."

"We'll be at your place in a minute. I'm just taking another way to make sure everything's all right." He glances over at Paulette and smiles. "Anyway," he says, "do you think I'm going to turn down the opportunity to get you out in my car? I've been trying to get you in here almost a year now."

"Tell you what," Paulette says, even though she likes getting flirted with like this, "you're going to have to clean up your act before you ever get me in this old heap again. I don't like this kind of stuff one bit."

"Everything's going to be fine," he says. He still keeps his eyes on the mirror, watching. He knows how things can get going quick before a guy knows it, knows that a fellow can't ever be too careful in a situation like this.

In the hospital Ronnie lays in a bed with his arm in a cast and his butt feeling like somebody has taken a hammer and driven some nails into it. From what he can remember some guy who maybe was a doctor stood by the bed and told him he had a broken elbow and some heavy bruising in his pelvic area, which Ronnie took to mean he had really got his ass busted this time in numerous places. He barely recalled this conversation and was for a while wondering if he'd simply dreamed it, but when he looks he sees the cast and he looks around and sees he's in a room, and there's no damn denying how bad his ass feels. It's so bad that he decides to postpone getting out of bed and trying to get to the restroom to take a piss, because, one, he's dizzy as hell and probably doped up with something, and two, he's got a pretty good idea that every single part and section of his body is going to hurt like hell ten times as much as it does now if he dares to make a move.

So this truly sucks. He has to lay here and maybe wet the bed while he wonders when the cops are going to come in and arrest him and haul him off to jail. He wonders if they're going to let him get a little better first or if they'll just come in and load him up in a van like he's a sack of shit. He tries not to consider it too much, but he wonders if he's even going to get better, if this shit he's feeling is permanent or not. He does his best to look at the ceiling and not think too much about dying. God, he keeps thinking, I've really fucked myself up for good this time.

As soon as he sees Ray drive off with Lillian and Lee, Trent takes one quick loop around the store to see how many customers there are in the aisles. He's happy to see there's only one person shopping, a woman in her pajama pants who probably clocks in at two hundred and eight-five pounds with her kid who could play Pugsley in the Addams Family, who is at the other end of the aisle from her and yells, "Hurry up!" at her like they need to get this done so they can get back to the trailer and tend to the meth lab they've got cooking tonight. Goddamn if he's going to wait around for this piece of trash to get finished filling up her cart, Trent thinks. He'll get her out of here right quick.

He goes up into the office and tells Fred to get ready to lock everything up, then he picks up the microphone and speaks into it at a decibel close to a shout.

"Bubba, lock up that back door and let's go home before we all get snowed in."

There's nobody at the back door and there is no Bubba, but

this is one of those tricks Trent has learned to spook tardy customers and scare them into thinking they are about to get locked up inside the store with no way to get out. Of course, viewing mother and son back in the aisle like he has, Trent figures getting locked in the store overnight might be a desirable type of alternative, considering the pig sty the two probably live in with maybe eight or nine others. But there's always that meth lab to take care of, so he thinks there's a good chance he might get them moving to the front registers pretty fast.

"Come on, Mama," Pugsley hollers. "They're fixing to lock the doors. We've got to hurry up and get out of here."

"You just hold your damn horses," the woman says. "I told you I didn't want you coming with me in the first place, so don't you be trying to make me get in a rush over you. I don't give a damn what you want to do when you get home."

"I want to see if they've called off school yet."

"Whether you go to school or not, you ain't going to be lying around getting in my way all day. I ain't going to have it. I got things I need to do. I ain't got time to fool with you. If it snows you can just go outside and bury yourself in it all day."

Maybe, Trent thinks, this getting these two out of the store isn't going to be so easy after all. He may have to resort to more drastic measures just so he can get closed up and get out of here. He walks over to the switchbox on the office wall and starts flicking off lights. He'll see how much shopping these two can do in the dark.

Martha is not having any trouble at all getting home, and she wonders what all the fuss has been about. She's less than a mile from her house now and hasn't had the first bit of trouble, no slips or slides or spinning wheels whatsoever. She sees Pete's headlights on the cruiser behind her and she starts to pick up her phone and tell him she is fine and he can go on about his business, but there is the little thought in the corner of her mind that the minute she does tell him that and he leaves her to go the rest of the way home then that is when she will drive her Subaru off into a ditch and be stuck out on the road waiting for him to come back and help her. She's so close now she thinks it is probably wise to keep him nearby just in case. Why chance it now? May as well play it safe. She does wonder why Pete has made such a point of following her home tonight. It isn't like she is such a terrible driver that he has to worry about her all the time, even in weather like this, since she hasn't come close to having a wreck for at least twenty years. She has a flashy trace of a fear that maybe he has sniffed out something about Trent and her and is planning on confronting her about it when they get home, but the idea of that seems far-fetched and unfeasible the more she thinks about it. How could he know anything, she asks herself? Could he have seen them together somewhere? Has someone told him anything? She doesn't see how. She and Trent have never gone out anywhere in public, and absolutely no one knows anything about them seeing each other, so probably she is just having a small wave of guilt or nervous regret over what's been going on. She doesn't really think that anything is up, but she knows she needs to be careful all the time anyway. She also knows that if she continues to have these kinds of paranoid feelings and can't enjoy herself because of it she'll drop Trent Collier like he's going out of style. She'll be through with that boy in a heartbeat, because, and she doesn't mind facing it, he's not worth the trouble. He may think he's hot stuff and God's gift to women, but he's really not.

She pulls into the driveway and turns on the garage door opener, watching Pete in the mirror to see if he's going to go back to work now or follow her inside for a minute. The lights on the cruiser go off, so she knows that means he's coming inside. Maybe he's hungry and he wants to have a little snack before he goes back to work.

She certainly hopes that's all it is. She's tired. She's had a long day. She doesn't need any knock-down, drag-outs with him tonight. What she needs is to go to bed. She's not even going to watch the news. The snow has pretty much stopped. End of story. Tomorrow comes early. Tomorrow is another day. She has to go to work again.

He is already in the kitchen when she comes in through the laundry room, but he isn't in the refrigerator looking for anything, but merely standing there with a glass of water in his hand waiting for her. All at once this doesn't look good to her, and once again she wonders if he knows something about her and Trent that he hasn't been letting on.

"I'll bet you had a rough day," he says. "At least that's the way it looked every time I passed by the place. It looked like you guys were getting worn out."

"We were. Of course that's the way it is when it snows. People lose their minds."

"They don't act that way up north," he smiles. "Up there something like we had today wouldn't have even been considered a real storm."

"Are you off for the night or do you have to go back in? I

thought you were going to have to work a double shift or something."

"I have to go back in," he says, "but it's not like it's going to be that busy now. What snow we've got is enough to keep everybody in for the rest of the night. But I thought I'd take a little break before I go back to work."

He first noticed it this morning when he came in for his doughnuts and he thought he'd gotten it out of his system when he stopped in and visited Betty Hutcherson on his way home, but that didn't seem to do it. Maybe it was the snow that was invigorating him this way—he's not sure. He hasn't slept that much, so it can't be that he's totally rested and that's why he's feeling his oats so. He has to go ahead and admit it's Martha doing this to him. He can go a while and take or leave her, but there always seems to come a time when he takes a look at her and suddenly he gets all worked up over her just like that, and then the only thing left to do is follow through on it, although sometimes now it seems to surprise her a little, like she doesn't expect him to ever show her any attention ever again.

And tonight when he ran Ray's kid by he saw Martha scuttling around getting things done so she could leave, and there was something in the way she walked around moving her body that caught his eye and made him think how it was sort of stupid for him to go traipsing all over the goddamn town looking for action when he's got a woman looks like this right there in his own house, better than anything out there in Sullivan he might be taking a look at. So he thought right then he'd just follow her back home and make sure she got in safe, and while he was there—well, here he is and there she is. So it feels like he's had a good idea about something after all.

He walks toward her before she can even get her coat off. He can hardly wait to get his hands on her. It's weird is what it is, this feeling, but it comes over him sometimes. Sometimes there's not a damn thing he can do to stop it.

Before Martha has time to even think about it, Pete's hands are on her and they are kissing in the kitchen and she doesn't know whether she likes it or not. She wants to not like it and to tell him to stop, but in a minute she realizes she does like it and she's an easy mark and she doesn't know whether to be mad at herself or not. Her head is spinning and she feels a hot rush through her body. Suddenly she doesn't feel so tired anymore. It's as if the day hasn't happened. It's like there has not been a snow rush or a thirteen hour day and what happened during the night with Trent didn't go on at all. All at once it's easy to forget everything, especially Trent, and go with the flow of the here and now. This hasn't happened in a while with Pete, she thinks, and maybe she should pay attention because her heart is pounding and her blood is rushing and she hasn't felt like this in an awfully long time.

Ray doesn't know whether to totally light into Lee the minute Lee gets back in the car from escorting Lillian to her door. There's a part of him that keeps telling him to stay silent and let the lack of conversation sink in on Lee that way. Maybe that might be the answer, he wonders. God knows he's chewed Lee's ass out for so many things so many times here in the last year or so that a change of strategy might be the best thing to do. Maybe it has just got to the point between Lee and him that whatever he says goes unheard and is a waste of breath and time. Maybe instead of stirring the pot so much he should just let the boy stew for a while.

But destruction of private property? Driving under the influence of something? Ray is no expert, but he'd bet his bottom dollar Lee's smoking pot if nothing else. He's seen it too many times with the in the door out the door part-time kids at the store. Most of them can't make it into work a week at a time because they're stoned out of their gizzards by the time they get home from school. So why should he believe Lee might be different? Ray hasn't seen anything from Lee over the past couple of years that tells him his son is any better than the rest of the kids in this town. He hates to admit it, but probably Lee is worse. He probably makes most of these kids look like stellar citizens.

He drives and waits for Lee to say something. It looks like the snow has stopped.

Lillian gets inside the house and changes into her nightgown. Actually it is not much of a gown at all but is more like a gigantic moo-moo that engulfs her skinny body but keeps her good and warm while she putters around the house. Since Johnny died fifteen years ago she hasn't done much to change this old rat-trap, but has just let it stay the same while she worked and came home and watched television and gossiped on the phone and chain-smoked cigarettes. It hasn't been much of a life and she knows it. She's seventy-one and keeps telling herself she is going to retire real soon, but she can't say when. She doesn't really know what she would do if she did. She wouldn't have people coming in to see her at the store. There wouldn't be anybody listening to what she had to say. She's afraid she'd just sit at home alone all day and night, and she isn't ready for that kind of solitude yet.

She's afraid she has cancer on top of everything else, but she doesn't want to go to the doctor just yet. She thinks maybe the way she feels will pass.

Trice spots the car coming in the opposite direction as he's coming up to make a left on Paulette's street. His first impulse is to speed up and try to outrace whoever it is looking for him, but he decides to take it easy and act like nothing is wrong and take Paulette home. He hopes like hell the people in the car don't recognize him since they're going in the opposite direction. Maybe he can pass them and they'll keep on going down the road.

This all changes when he sees the brake lights turn red and the car come to a stop, so he knows he's been spotted and the car is turning around to come after him. He tells himself this is the time to stop play-acting like nothing is wrong and get himself into gear. He can see Paulette looking at him as he speeds up and passes her street, so he knows he's got to let her know something—he doesn't know exactly what—is fixing to go down.

"I've got to haul my ass out of here," he tells her. "I can't stop and let you out right now. I've got somebody after me and it looks like they ain't playing."

He's afraid to go all out on his speed because of what snow is on the street and because his tires are getting close to bald too, but he gets way above the speed limit anyway and hopes he doesn't do anything stupid to wreck the car. What he's thinking is he can get on the back streets here and make some turns and backtrack a little and lose this other car. He's a pretty good driver, so maybe he can twist and turn and get out of this situation. Paulette is sitting straight up in her seat holding on to the strap above the door with one hand and bracing herself against the dashboard with the other. He's pretty sure she's going to start yelling at him any second now.

"I'll get us out of this," he tells her before she can speak. "I promise nothing will happen. I'll have you home in a couple of minutes."

He feels like he's in a movie or inside a video game with all the turns and speeding up and slowing down they're doing. A few times he goes into a skid and starts sliding around sideways some, but he manages to straighten the car out and keep on going. He runs through a flashing red light at about forty and makes a quick left down a road that runs across the street from the store, so at least he knows where he is and can come up with some sort of plan to get away. In his mirror he sees something happening behind him and the headlights begin getting smaller the farther down the road he goes, and suddenly he is alone on the road again. The other car is nowhere to be seen. He wants to go back and see what's happened but thinks that's a stupid idea. Best for him to keep going. Get Paulette home and find some place to make himself scarce for the rest of the night.

He looks over and sees Paulette has a pistol in her hand. Damn girl is packing—he would have never thought it.

"If anybody gets too close to us I'm going to shoot their ass and ask questions later," she says.

Larry is close to being home when he sees Trice's car run through the light and the car that was at the store earlier come flying through after him and run straight into a panel truck for a plumbing company. His first impulse is to run over and see if anybody is hurt, but the way that car was hanging around the store a while back and the way Trice was trying to get away from it makes him hesitate a minute and stay where he is and let somebody else get over there first. He wants to see what happens when somebody gets out of the car. He can see who is driving and who is in there, and maybe he can let Trice know if he's still in trouble or not. He knows one thing already—whoever is in the car isn't going to be going anywhere in the damn thing for a while, maybe forever, because that son of a bitch is totaled if he's ever seen such a thing before.

It's been a minute and nobody has got out of the car yet. The driver in the panel truck is out and on a cell phone, and Larry can already hear the whine of a siren off in the distance, so he knows the cops are on the way. Better bring an ambulance too, he thinks. Somebody in that car is bound to be hurt.

There's a small crowd beginning to gather—people from the houses around the intersection and men driving home from work who stop and see if there's any blood and guts for them to look at. Larry tries to blend in a little so he's not picked out by one of the cops who are showing up and run in on suspicion of something. Larry knows he hasn't done anything to be worried about, but being innocent hasn't ever stopped the police from hassling him before, so it's best to be careful. Anyway, there's always that reefer he's got in his sock. They'd find that first thing and he'd be up the creek without a fucking paddle.

In about five minutes a fire truck has shown up and four paramedics are surrounding the car. Two guys go at it with the

Jaws of Life and start working on the door, so Larry knows the guy in there is either dead or seriously fucked up or can't get the car door open. Whatever the case is, it's obvious Trice is safe tonight. If Larry had a cell phone he'd call him and let him know, but he doesn't, so Trice will have to figure it out himself. If he shows up for work tomorrow he'll tell him then.

The medics open the door and get this one guy out and put him on a stretcher. Larry's about twenty yards away, so it's hard to tell if the dude is dead or not. One thing is for sure--he ain't moving. The truck takes off with its red lights turning around in circles and its siren blaring, so Larry knows the show is over for now. He takes off walking again. His place is just over the hill. He notices how the snow has completely stopped. All that fucking work today for nothing, he thinks. He wonders about the dude with the check who got splattered in front of the store—maybe he's dead too. I go to work in the morning and before I get home there are maybe two people who've got killed right in front of me—this goes through his mind as he steps in little drifts of snow while a west wind tries to work its way down his coat collar. He could do with a little heavier jacket than what he's got.

Ray keeps waiting. He's thinking if he's silent long enough Lee will finally speak, maybe even—miracle above miracles—offer an apology and state how he will try not to do such dumbass things on a regular basis so much in the future. Having thoughts like this almost give Ray the inclination to glance out the window and see if a band of heavenly hosts are on the way down from on high to transform this world of sorry behavior and woe into something shiny and radiant and worthy for choirs of angels to sing about, but he doesn't scan the horizon too awfully long because he knows there isn't going to be anything there for him to see.

"Man, this is all screwed up, isn't it?"

Lee has spoken. He sits on his side fingering the sun visor to keep from lighting up another cigarette, since he already knows his dad doesn't want anybody smoking in his car and just got through having Miss Lillian and him doing it at the same time, so if he lights up again now he's going to get yelled at about that too. Lee doesn't need anything else to go on for his dad to go off about. There's enough already.

"You bet it's screwed up," Ray says. "I wonder whose fault that is."

"I didn't mean to tear that hill up," Lee says. "I was just in a hurry to get home. I was afraid the snow was going to get deep and I wouldn't be able to make it to the house."

"You must have been in a real hurry. You left work and didn't tell anybody you were leaving. I guess you were so worried about the storm that you forgot."

"I'd already worked my entire shift, Dad. I don't think it's so bad for a guy to go home from work on time. There wasn't anything there for me to do but bag. Everybody else was up there taking care of that."

"We were busy, Lee. This is a business. When it gets like that we need everybody helping. It was an emergency situation."

"It turns out it didn't snow that much, so it really didn't matter."

"It could have."

They are almost home, so Lee doesn't think he ought to wait any longer to ask.

"Are you going to take me to get my car? It's still sitting in that parking lot out there by itself. Somebody's liable to try and steal it."

"You don't know the answer to that already?" Rays says, trying to keep his voice down or clenching his teeth so hard they break up like icy little Chiclets. "You embarrass the hell out of me at the store and you almost get your tail arrested and you're going to cost me who knows how much money, and now you want me to drive you to get your car. For what? So you can go back out tonight and do something stupid in it again? No thanks, mister. You can come home with me and spend a night there for a change. Maybe tomorrow morning I'll drive you back out there to get your car, but if you want it tonight you can walk."

"I can get somebody else to take me," Lee says sullenly. "It's no big deal to me."

"I've got your keys," Ray says. "Martha's husband gave them to me." He smiles at his son. For the first time in a while Ray is the winner, and he sort of likes it. He decides to finish the kid off, for this night at least.

"Unless you've got a spare set," he tells him, "it looks to me like you're shit out of luck."

Trice can't see anything behind him anymore; it's like he and Paulette are alone on the streets. He guesses everybody has made it home by now and is afraid to come out anymore because of the snow, but he's got news for everybody if they haven't got eyes to look out their window and see for themselves—there ain't much white stuff on the street. Maybe an inch, he relents, but nothing more than that. All that bullshit they went through all day long was for nothing. And whoever was chasing him, well, they're gone too. He doesn't know what happened back there, but it's for damn sure it's going to be a while before he goes back to see.

He pulls up to the curb in front of Paulette's place and waits to see how fast she gets out. She lives in the side of a small duplex where there's just one window facing the street. The rest look over to the house next door where there's never a light or a car to be seen but which has a pit bull-looking dog hanging out behind a fence that raises hell anytime Paulette gets home from work or if anybody comes to pick her up and give her a ride somewhere. Trice has never been up the sidewalk to Paulette's door, nor has she ever invited him in, but he wants her to do just that tonight. It's not that he's all that horny so much—not any more than ever, that is—but there was something tonight that halfway got to him like things generally never get to him, semi-scared him with the way whoever was in that car kept circling the store and following him like they weren't ever going to give up until they found him. He wonders what he's done to illicit a response like that from somebody, and he thinks maybe he needs to watch what he does a little more and be careful. While he was driving fast on what ice there was it came into his head that if he got caught and worse came to worse and somebody plugged him and that was it for him then there wasn't going to be anybody much who would miss him if he wasn't around. He's never thought of his life like that before, him just being dead and in the grave and the world going on without it mattering much at all, and so now he wouldn't mind doing something about it. He wonders about Paulette, who never seems to have anybody much too. She'll tell you she don't need any man, don't need anybody, but sometimes Trice can take a look at her when she's saying such things and he don't half believe her. He thinks maybe Paulette may need somebody too, that maybe she's had the same kind of thing pass through her head before too. This is something he'd like to find out.

But besides all that, he's not all that crazy to go back to his apartment right now. He doesn't know if anybody might be there waiting on him or not. He doesn't want to go back and learn the answer. He wouldn't mind staying right here a while. Paulette has a gun too, and she seems to know how to use it. That could be another plus to the equation.

"I don't know what you've got going on, but you sure as shooting need to do something to get yourself clear of it." Paulette sits in her seat without opening the door, giving Trice this look that's about half disgust and the other half concern. "I don't know what to do about you," she says.

"I'm going to try and get better," he tells her. "I'm going to do my best to put all this stuff behind me."

Pete and Martha haven't even gotten in bed good when his phone starts going off on the dresser. Since he's supposed to be on duty and not making love to his wife he has no choice but to answer it, so he goes and reports back and gets informed of the bad wreck at Lewis and Woodard, how he needs to get over there for assistance because there are injuries and possible life-threatening situations.

"I have to go," he tells Martha. He is not happy about this.

"I know you do," she says. "Be careful."

More than that fire in her body that she hasn't felt in a while—not even the past month with Trent—she is relieved to see him go. More than this night and what almost happened, she has a lot of thinking to do. She needs to think and get it out of the way and get some sleep. She has to be back at work in the morning.

Trent makes it to his apartment and climbs the steps to his floor, watching where he's walking because there's a little ice here and there. Nothing bad, though. Nothing like everybody thought it was going to be like this morning. Mostly the whole shebang had been nothing but a false alarm, a lot of worry and panic over something that didn't occur and hardly ever does in this town or state where snow is a seldom-seen oddity.

He can watch the news or see if there's a movie on he hasn't seen. There's beer in the refrigerator, but he doesn't want one. He makes a sandwich with some bologna and cheese and opens a bag of chips. He pours some Pepsi he hopes hasn't gone flat yet and sits down at the breakfast bar. He doesn't turn on the TV but studies the patterns in the wallpaper that, if he looks at them long enough, appear to be clowns' faces. Welcome to the circus, he thinks.

He doesn't know what he's going to do but it isn't this. When he goes in to work tomorrow afternoon the first thing he's going to do is hand in a resignation letter to Ray. He doesn't know exactly how he's going to word it yet, since it just came to him this very minute, and he doesn't know what he's going to do after he leaves, but it's for absolute certain he doesn't want to do this for the rest of his goddamn life. He doesn't want to be in charge of a bunch of kids down in the hood. He doesn't want to get the shit beaten out of him or get killed by Martha's old man. He doesn't even want to stay in this town anymore.

He can move back to Kingsport and stay with his mother a

while. She'll either hate it or love it—it's hard to tell how she'll react to him showing up again. But it will work for a while. It's not like it has to be permanent. He'll just buy a little time to see where he wants to go next. Whatever, it's got to beat this scene. Anything's better than this.

Pete pulls in with his lights flashing just as the paramedics are taking off. He gets out and watches the ambulance drive past the intersection and head for the hospital, then he walks over to see what has happened.

They're transporting the driver to the hospital," Bobby tells him. "He was the only one in the car." He points at the mangled car in the middle of the intersection, its front end pushed all the way to the back seat. "Rammed head-on into that van. That guy's all right. He's on his feet and answering questions. Wasn't his fault, looks like to me. Ain't no hurry getting to the hospital, though. The paramedics don't need to take any chances on the road. That guy's dead as a doornail.

NINE
10:00 P.M.

Ronnie does his best to fake being unconscious for most of the evening, but he finally gives up trying after the two cops—one man, one woman—come in for about the twentieth time to tell him they know who he is and read him his rights. He learns he's under arrest for a bunch of stuff and he can have an attorney if he wants, but he just closes his eyes when they leave, figuring when he opens them again he'll either be on his way or in jail already. So he guesses he'll just wait and see what happens in the morning. It doesn't take much to be patient when you're fucked up like this. It's not like he is going to get up and go anywhere. He's going to be here in this hospital or locked up somewhere for a while, so there's no need in getting all hot and bothered about it. Because there's nothing he can do about it.

Larry gets inside the halfway house and signs himself in for the night. Nobody really checks the register much and it's not a big deal if he doesn't write his name down, but he's seen enough of this day and decides it will be better for him to be careful. He's seen a dude get wasted and another one maybe die, and he doesn't know if there's still anybody out there after

Trice anymore or not. He can wait and find out about that tomorrow. After everything this day he's just glad to get back to his room. He's glad it didn't snow. He won't have any trouble walking to work in the morning now.

Derrick is watching an NBA game on the TV in his bedroom. He's in bed with a can of Bud Lite, a little high from the joint he had on the way home. He's not really all that fucked up, but every few minutes he has to try and focus in on which teams are playing. He keeps getting them mixed up, the cities and the uniforms. It's all right, though. It's not like he really gives a shit. He starts to call Trice and see if he got home okay, but he doesn't. It's not like he gives much of a shit about that either. He's cool here in his room. He doesn't need any of the bullshit drama going on out there in the night.

Pete drives around for a while and thinks about going back home, but that moment seems to have passed now. It's the way things are with him these days. He gets the impulse to do something and the next thing he knows something has come up and he's back out in the middle of it again. It's why he has to go and do what he needs to whenever he gets the chance, otherwise he's liable to wind up doing nothing at all. He's been a cop a lot of years now, and he still never knows what's going to happen next.

Martha keeps thinking she'll drift off to sleep but she doesn't. She lays in bed thinking about Pete and Trent and wondering what exactly is going on with her these days. What is she doing? A part of her thinks she must be asking for trouble, but she is sure that's not really it. Maybe it's just all these years of going to work and coming home, being in two places most of the time, one husband who's sometimes there and sometimes not, and finding her a lover like in books or on the afternoon soaps that makes things different in some way, but when she lays here like this she's not so certain she wants anything that's different anymore. It's hard to not know what you ought to do next all the time. Sometimes it's better to just live your life with as little worry as possible.

Lillian stubs out a cigarette and takes her three pills before she goes to bed. One for her heart, one for acid reflux, one for depression. She takes a pill at supper for blood sugar, an allergy pill and a couple of aspirins in the morning, chews two or three antacids during the day. She starts to feed the cat, and then she remembers she hasn't seen the cat in almost a week now. She keeps looking for that little devil, thinking he'll come back. She keeps thinking she'll hear him at the door. She looks out the window and sees there isn't much snow to speak of. She hasn't decided if she'll go to work tomorrow or not. She'll have to see how she feels in the morning. If she doesn't, she can always get someone to take her to get her car later on.

Bob Howell drinks his last beer when the news comes on, waiting to see what the weather is going to be like tomorrow. He's had his usual six beers sitting on a stool and watching the TV above the bar. He's careful on the way home like he always is. He keeps a sharp eye out for cops. He doesn't need another DUI. He knows the third one will be strike three.

Lyle's been home from his deacons' meeting twenty minutes. He peels a banana and eats it before he goes to bed. His wife is in the basement doing laundry. He doesn't tell her he's home, but just waits in the kitchen to see if she'll jump when she opens the door and sees him. For a little bit he'd call

Marcus and Shirley and tell them to come in early tomorrow. With the case wiped out and empty and a truck coming in, there's going to be a lot to do. The trouble is he knows them both too good. They're liable to think about all that has to be done and call out sick to keep from facing all that work, so it's better not to say anything at all.

Paulette has allowed Trice to come inside, but she'd told him straight up she isn't going to tolerate any of his monkey business. I don't want you to get shot, so you can sleep on the sofa out there by the TV, but that's as far as it goes. She'd shut her bedroom door and turned out the light, and for fifteen minutes Trice sits and watches TV and wonders if he ought to try something or not. Does Lillian really want him to? He has to think about it some more. The last thing she'd done before she went to bed was remind him she had a gun. I'll use it if I have to, she told him. He wonders about her saying something like that and which way he ought to take it.

But at least he is inside the door, and he figured that was a start.

Lee decides it's just a fucked-up night and he's good and fucked-up too to go along with it. He wonders how long his dad is going to keep his keys and how long he's going to have to stay on the shit list until his dad decides he's paid for the property damage and learned a lesson on top of it. It could be weeks. He wishes he could get over to his car right now someway, because he could at least get the rest of his joint out of the car and sneak a few hits around the house while everybody was asleep. Maybe he can at least do that tomorrow, because they have to move the car out of that lot sometime. Maybe he can do it then.

Ray can't go right to bed, so he sits up in bed looking at a Sports Illustrated while his wife reads a copy of Southern Living. He's not so sure she knows about Lee and his car yet, because he for sure hasn't told her, but he doesn't want to ask because he's pretty sure she'll enable the kid and drive him down there to keep him from worrying about somebody stealing it. Ray knows already there's going to be a big argument about Lee and the car and everything. He doesn't look forward to it. It's not going to be pretty at all.

Trent looks at his resignation letter and folds it once and places it by his car keys and wallet. It seems almost anticlimactic now, this act, like there is something else he should do but has forgotten. He thinks about calling Martha and telling her so it won't come as so big of a shock to her, but he doesn't want to do that tonight. It will be better to wait. He doesn't want to talk to her tonight or hear what she has to say. He guesses that will happen soon enough.

Maybe.

There's a chance she'll never say a word about it. He could work this last two weeks and leave and the whole thing would never be discussed. She could make it like it never happened. That doesn't seem right to him, but one way or another he guesses he'll see.

By midnight Valentine's Day is a thing of the past. Warm air from the south has moved in, bringing more clouds filled with rain. It is like winter had to take its leave very fast, like it couldn't stick around because spring was right behind it, early, and spring, false and unpunctual as it was, now was blowing in for a day or two and snow wasn't welcome here. The snow had to go somewhere else.

It began to rain. The warm rain melted what leftover traces of snow there was, and by early morning the streets of Sullivan were clear.

THE END